BRAND FIRES ON THE RIDGE

BRAND FIRES ON THE RIDGE

Ernest Haycox

Thorndike Press • Chivers Press
Thorndike, Maine USA   Bath, Avon, England

This Large Print edition   .ed by Thorndike Press, USA and by Chivers Press, England.

Published in 1995 in the U.S. by arrangement with the Golden West Literary Agency.

Published in 1995 in the U.K. by arrangement with the Golden West Literary Agency.

U.S. Hardcover   0-7862-0347-1 (Western Series Edition)
U.K. Hardcover   0-7451-2929-3 (Chivers Large Print)
U.K. Softcover   0-7451-2933-1 (Camden Large Print)

The text of this Large Print edition is unabridged.
Other aspects of the book may vary from the original edition.

Set in 16 pt. News Plantin.

Printed in Great Britain on acid-free paper.

British Library Cataloguing in Publication Data available

Library of Congress Cataloging in Publication Data

Haycox, Ernest, 1899–1950.
    Brand fires on the ridge / Ernest Haycox.
        p.   cm.
    ISBN 0-7862-0347-1 (alk. paper : lg. print)
    1. Large type books. I. Title.
[PS3515.A9327B73 1995]
813'.52—dc20   94-32530

Contents

BRAND FIRES ON THE RIDGE

Chapter One

When, as the afternoon shadows began to pitch farther ahead of horse and rider, King Merrick came up the gentle rise of the road and passed the towering shaft of Fire Rock he also passed a boundary line. And in celebration of the event he drew rein, hooked a leg over the saddle horn and rolled himself a cigarette, meanwhile looking ahead with a slow, pleased smile. The boundary was imaginary. Strictly speaking, there was no legal division of territory hereabouts needing a boundary line and none was recognized save by those who lived southward beyond Fire Rock. But to the inhabitants thereof it was as plain as if a tremendous chalk mark had been scored across the earth at this point and to them it was the front door of home. South was "The Valley." North was "outside."

The valley, fresh and sparkling under the

hot sun, lay between pine clad ridges that bowed outward from a common origin at Fire Rock and closed again in the distance, merging with a mass of higher, more rugged hills. The valley thus created was something like twelve or fifteen miles in length and at its widest point no more than four miles broad. A road and a river split it. To either side of this cleavage were lesser trails and creeks sidling into the bench lands and to the cattle ranches thereon. From this vantage point King Merrick could distinguish some of the nearer outfits, their home houses and corrals. Occasionally along the winding and the lengthening of the road he made out stock crossing and recrossing. Meadows, emerald green, lay like patterns between rows and groves of trees. One single spiral of smoke rose to the sun. Abruptly King dropped his cigarette and urged the pony on, impatient to be among old friends and old things.

"They're out already, hazin' the critters from the brush," he told his horse. "Blamed if I can't about smell scorched hide. I stayed away pretty near too long. Hustle, pony."

And though King had traveled a great distance that day, he put the horse to a lope. So into the valley they went, a small glass-eyed calico horse as ugly as sin carrying a typical man of the range — not extraordinarily tall nor extraordinarily heavy. There were a thousand men in cattle country like King Merrick, with the same bronzed and slightly sharpened features and with the same roving blue-gray eyes. Still, a dozen different aspects of his personality crept out to defy an exact classification. At first glance he seemed only of average strength as physical strength is measured among horsemen. A closer and more experienced eye would have caught the possibilities of King Merrick's full-arched chest and the compact coupling of neck and shoulders. Sitting in the saddle after a long journey he seemed a figure of lazy indifference and he wore his hat at an angle, a perfect picture of a rider who would sweat and labor the weary summer months for wages and spend all in a single night's wild foray. A man who was headstrong and reckless and cheerfully cynical. But yet when his glance fastened upon some familiar landmark of the valley the picture changed completely. Below the surface of those gray-blue eyes smouldered an affection and wistfulness that others almost never saw. King Merrick was a competent hand, and he kept himself well reined-in.

Down the road horse and rider went, past

locust and poplar, with cattle tracks marking the damp highway and the scent of pine and sage and fresh spring grasses rolling strongly up to his nostrils. The green and white ranch mail boxes marked the miles, each with its brand, burned deeply in the wood. King read them, though he could have closed his eyes and run through the roll. Then, about three quarters of the way down the valley's length, he drew in before a box and gravely announced name and brand to the horse.

"Mister Pack MacGabriel — Music Box outfit. If I had a nickel for every time I went past this box, pony, I'd be rich. Proceed leisurely but don't lose any time." They turned at right angles and followed a lesser road in the direction of the eastern ridge, climbing gradually.

About six of the evening King Merrick drew rein before Music Box home quarters, stepped stiffly to the ground and grinned. "Well, the sheriff ain't seized the premises yet. But I wonder if I still got a job?"

He had only a moment to wait in finding the answer. Pack MacGabriel ducked through the house door, a tall and gaunt Southerner with prominent cheekbones and a lank neck sagging against an immense Adam's apple. Pack had been crippled by horses years ago and ran his ranch from an arm chair. He owned a habitually severe face and he looked across the top rim of his steel spectacles at the new arrival without the least trace of welcome or pleasure. King Merrick's grin broadened.

"Howdy, Pack," he greeted. "Forgot to tell you last fall they was a rotten fence up at number two cabin. Figured I'd better drop in and let you know."

"You homely, dime-sized no-'count," grunted Pack. "So you went away from Music Box? I wondered why things run so smooth and peaceful around here this winter. Come to think about it, I dunno's I ever had a more shif'less riding boss than you was."

"Well, don't forget about that rotten fence post," King went on unperturbed. "Better have your new ridin' boss put another in. Providin' said ridin' boss can find his way through the pines without gettin' lost. This outfit always did have a haywire crew."

"Yuh?" challenged MacGabriel. "Mebbe you think you'd ought to put that post in?"

"Who, me?" King asked as though surprised. "Say, I got some pride. I'm particular where I work. Only reason I stuck around here last year was I felt like a man ought to do some charity once in a while. Any cow outfits in this country, Mister MacGabriel, or ain't there nothin' but chicken ranches, like this one?"

"That sounds natural," opined MacGabriel, smiling. He held out his raw-boned fist. "Glad to see you back, King."

King took the hand and gripped it tight. "Same to you, Pack."

"Was some worried you wasn't comin' back from outside," went on MacGabriel. "I sort of held back on roundup a few days. They's a spare peg in the bunkhouse, King. Wash up, and I'll listen to some more of your dam' lies. If I'd found anybody else fit to run this ranch I'd of hired him. Seeing as I didn't, I guess you're still in command."

"I'll take the job until the sheriff forecloses," said King cheerfully. "Where's the boys?"

"Draggin' the near stuff out of Section Line wash. Like I said, I sort of held up roundup, figurin' you'd pull in a little late. It's our second day. Dusty's been in charge. All right, we're set to go. In the mornin' you lay on the bull whip. Dam' rascals need a proddin'."

King nodded. "Soon as I load my britches full of staples and find a milk bucket and a pair of pliers I'll try to renovate a bad situation."

"Boys comin' in now."

The Music Box crew spurred into sight, straggling across a meadow and around a clump of jack pines. They saw King Merrick from afar and of a sudden the group of horses drew into a compact knot and swept along the road, into the yard and down upon the newcomer. He was made the target of good-natured epithets and ribald questions that would have shamed a man less accustomed to the country.

"Hey, look what got through the front gate! Say, King, did yuh buy me them ten yards o' petticoat lace I asked for?" called one red-faced rider.

"Haw — he prob'ly bought it aw'right an' give it to a dancin' dolly in Rawlins," somebody else spoke up.

"Shucks, he never got to Rawlins. He don't look thin enough to've rid that fur."

"Thasso? Hell, that Joe could go around the world on a nickel and come back seal-fat. He's so tight he'd make a bass drum sound like a piccolo."

"Oh, fa-la-la! What'm I goin' to do fur petticoat lace? It jes' nacherlly annoys me to sleep in plain garments."

"Yuh ain't goin' to get any more sleep. The slave driver's back."

King Merrick eyed them derisively. "I've

sure heard a lot of jackasses bray, but you make more noise than most. Tomorra night you'll come home walkin' closer to the ground. Put that in the book. You been playin' cribbage all winter and soldierin' like a bunch of reservation Injuns. This place looks like the wrath of God swamped it."

The foremost rider fell out of his saddle and struck King a resounding blow on the chest. "It's a good thing I'm proof against poison ivy. King, yore a sight for granulated eyes!"

"Same to you, Dusty."

The range man reacts to sentiment. Mac-Gabriel turned inside the house while the rest of the punchers headed for the corral, leaving King and Dusty Tremaine alone. In this valley the staunch and deep-rooted friendship of the two men was a by word. Tremaine and Merrick habitually made a pair. Where one was the other naturally and inevitably gravitated. And so in the crowding twilight they faced each other over a lapse of three months, heads tipped back, saying nothing for the moment. For partners they were extraordinarily dissimilar. One was a compact and self-contained man, not given to display or fireworks. He was very apt to be a spectator on the edge of things until the showdown came. The other was a tall and lean giant with yellow hair and an exuberance of spirit that wasted itself on anything great or small. Dusty Tremaine loved excitement and battle whether it was over the poker table or in the corral. Where men laughed the loudest and chips clacked and the smoke rolled he loved to be. If there was some explosive horseplay afoot, Dusty Tremaine surely maneuvered himself to the center of the trickery. There was a quality of lovableness about Dusty Tremaine that drew others. He was of the kind who made friends hand over hand and whipped them into all manner of weird antics by the contagion of his rollicking nature. He was three or four inches taller than King, his eyes were a deeper blue and his face infinitely more mobile and expressive. King easily merged with a crowd and, except when a definite leadership was needed, he stayed there. But Dusty Tremaine stood out conspicuously, no matter how many were around him.

"Suppose you been leading these boy scouts into all sorts of hell," murmured King, smiling. "Scarin' widows and old men, but not doin' enough work to pay assessment."

"I'm dam' glad to turn this outfit over to you, and no mistake," said Dusty. He guffawed and put an arm around King's shoulders. "Come on, I want to tell you what we did with the Circle J's chuck wagon last Christmas. We went over after dark — "

"Yeah," King interrupted. "How many calves you find today?"

Dusty was vague. He waved a hand into the shadows. "Ask Slim Martis, he kep' track. I got hung up in the buck brush."

"What's new?" King asked.

"In the valley? You'd ought to know better. There ain't nothin' new."

"How about the Brierly boys?"

Dusty shrugged his shoulders. "Oh, same old stories. But what's the use of believin' everything yuh hear about 'em? Maybe they ain't so bad. You know I ain't a hand to pin gossip to folks and sometimes it sort of aggravates me to hear others manufacturin' suspicion. Sure does."

"Any more bereaved cows up in the hills, Dusty?"

"Some, I guess. I don't pay much attention."

They went the length of the yard before King Merrick mustered a patently casual question. "Expect maybe you've seen Lolita Spring now and again in town?"

Dusty was unsaddling. He threw a sober glance across his pony's back and bent to the cinch. "Uhuh." King Merrick waited for additional news but since none came he refused to press farther and turned his horse into the corral, lugging saddle and gear to the bunkhouse. The cook's triangle started a rush across the yard. When King came out of the bunkhouse he saw Dusty astride a fresh horse.

"Great snakes, Dusty, don't you like eatin'?" he asked in surprise.

Dusty was still sober. It seemed to King that his partner was ill at ease and at loss for words, an unusual situation. "Yup," grunted Dusty, "I got a date up the line. See you later, King. I want to tell yuh what we did to that Circle J chuck wagon." He spurred down the road.

King followed the crew to the supper table, smiling broadly at the familiar oil cloth. But though he was again the target of the crew he said nothing, eating leisurely, savoring the comfort of the old surroundings. Somebody at the end of the table jeered at this silence.

"Allus was a putrefied mummy. Reckon he's cookin' up a lot of grief fur tomorra. Whoa is me and whoa is us. If I didn't know Music Box couldn't get another top hand like me I believe I'd draw my wages."

Pack MacGabriel snorted. "I'd get rid of

you in a minute, Stoney, if you wasn't so far in debt to Music Box. How can a man smoke up forty dollars of tobacco money in one night?"

The crew dwelt upon the possibilities quite gravely and Slim Martis finally reached an agreeable conclusion. "Think Stoney's trainin' a band of hawsses to chew tobacco for a circus. At least I saw him sleepin' on the ground inside a corral full o' brutes behind the saloon at Five Echo two Sattidys ago."

"That's a dam' lie!" stormed Stoney. "When I sobered up nex' mornin' they wasn't a hawss in the corral. Mebbe I drink and mebbe I sleeps in a corral. But I got sense enough to keep from under hoofs."

The talk subsided. Presently a softly murmured phrase escaped from Stoney's end of the table. "King'd better save his breath aw'right. He mebbe'll need it in a tussle."

King raised his head. Pack MacGabriel stared angrily toward Stoney. Complete silence weighted the tongues of the rest of the group. "What're you boys cookin' up?" mildly demanded King.

But Stoney wouldn't answer and Slim Martis raised his palms like an Indian. "It's that forty dollars worth of tobacco he drunk, King."

King finished his meal and went back to

the bunkhouse. He was tired, but there was a call he had to make yet tonight and the prospect of it simmered in him, stirring up a small excitement. He shaved in the lamplight, put on a clean shirt and neck piece and went out to saddle a stout pony. There was another standing saddled by the bar. Slim Martis loitered near at hand, smoking a cigarette. King passed him a questioning glance and started down the road. Pack MacGabriel's summons drew him from his trail over to the house porch.

"Don't mean to be personal," apologized Pack, shifting in the chair, "but was you going in the general direction of Five Echo tonight?"

"Yeah."

"Think you'll be in Five Echo about nine o'clock? Just maybe be driftin' in and lookin' around?"

King bent forward to study the ranch owner's face. The man was asking a favor and issuing a command in a roundabout fashion. So King inclined his head. "I reckon."

MacGabriel's cigar slashed a pattern across the shadows. Slim Martis slid beside the steps. "All right," grunted MacGabriel, "you hit out and do like I told, Slim. And keep yore mouth shut in between stops."

"You boys are just naturally wallowin' in

mystification," observed King Merrick. "Better unload some weight before you bust a vest button."

Slim Martis set the pony about, speaking across his shoulder. "Don't rush none, King. Enjoy yore tobacco awhile. When this business is offen our chests it's a-roostin' on yores."

"Shut yore mouth, Slim," cut in Mac-Gabriel. "Yore gettin' to be as limber-tongued as Stoney. If he don't cinch up his mouth I'll salivate him. Dig out and don't make too much noise poundin' along the road. Take all short cuts. Say to the gentleman it's to be nine o'clock prompt in Five Echo. And for them to go straight to the hotel room without attractin' notice."

"Yeah," murmured Slim, fading into the outer shadows.

"See you in Five Echo at nine," said MacGabriel to King. "And don't say anything meanwhile."

"How can I," asked King, "when I don't know anything?"

"You'll know plenty around nine. We been waitin' till you got back. Things has come to a head around here and you got to do some simplifyin'. And listen, King: I want yore word you won't get discouraged none between now and nine and make up yore mind to pull freight."

"You got it," King assured him. "But what makes you think I'm easily discouraged?"

MacGabriel's shoulders rose and fell. The cigar burned brightly and King saw the man's eyes gleaming brilliant and hard in the reflected light. "It's my observation," drawled MacGabriel, "that life's got a cur'ous way of risin' to belt a man under the chin unexpected."

King wheeled the horse. "All of which I assume and digest for fifty a month and found." He lined out across a meadow, the purple dusk swirling around.

Chapter Two

King Merrick followed a trail worn deep by his own previous pilgrimages. He promptly dismissed from his mind the warning issued by Pack MacGabriel. The year was young, the tissues of the earth were reviving from a long winter's sleep and sending into the night plain signals of birth and growth. All this trembled on the wings of the soft warm wind — the scent of evergreens and grasses, the sound of night creatures underfoot, the brawling of a creek in flood. To his left hand lay the bench, massed in opaque shadows. Higher, the ridge tops cut a ragged silhouette against the shifting sky, and down the long course of a wooded canyon rolled the weird and wailing bark of a coyote. The moon was a sharp, silver sickle.

Yonder where the ridges began to cramp the valley again was the Bench S outfit. And there he was bound to see Lolita Spring.

For two years King Merrick had pressed his fortune with the lady. He hoped that on this heady evening he would have the answer for which she long had made him wait. Last fall after beef roundup Lolita had said lightly: "What will I do, King, live in a tent and wash clothes on the creek stones? You're the smartest man in the valley and old MacGabriel pays you a flunky's wages. Who breaks horses that others can't ride — who is it that the Brierly boys haven't dared to bully? You're too good-natured to realize how you stand with everybody. I'm tired of being an old maid. You go find a piece of land and put up a shanty with one window and one door. And I'll fill it with dishes and blankets and furniture from the Bench S. I'll even steal a milk cow from dad. It's time you owned your own brand."

On the strength of this King Merrick immediately established an option with a diamond ring that came down from previous generations of Merrick women, did some scouting among the rugged draws to the south of Five Echo — approaching dangerously near Brierly territory — and finally set forth upon his winter's wandering "outside."

Two items prevented King from being absolutely certain the bargain was sealed, his own humbleness and Lolita Spring's impulsive nature. She wore his ring, and even now after long months had intervened the image of that scene was clearly in his mind — Yet who was to know the changing currents of a woman's heart, especially the heart of Lolita Spring?

He forded a creek that touched his stirrups, seeing the blink of a house light. Bench S corrals flanked him, Bench S buildings lay to either side. Skirting a bunkhouse he passed between long arbors of grapes and reined before the Spring ranch house. The door stood open and he saw old Jastrow Spring rocking inside. Dropping to the ground, King heard a murmur of voices sliding out of the porch's darkest end. A chair squealed. Lolita Spring's voice, light and gay, arrested him.

"King!"

"The same," said King, smiling broadly. "Come out and give my poor eyes a treat."

Somebody else was with her. Lolita stepped into the patch of light flooding through the door — Lolita as of old, vivid and alluring and graceful. For the moment King forgot whoever else tarried in the shadows. Lolita's firm little hand met his own broad paw and rested in it a fleeting instant. All that King wanted to say, all that he had planned to say stuck in his throat. He wasn't that kind of a man. So he murmured, "Glad to see you, Lolita. Got some news that maybe will interest you."

"Any news will interest me. The valley never turns up excitement. I can tell you everything that's happened since you were gone in one breath. A calf broke its leg and dad shot it. Old man Dunkery got drunk again. We've had two dances, and it's been a white winter. There — you have it all." She tilted her chin to inspect him, back to the light. He saw only the outline of her face and the white blur of her features. It stirred him immeasurably to have her study him thus. A small laugh caught up the shadows and wove a pattern through them. "Oh, King, what is it about you that seems to steady people? Old faithful, old dependable." She turned and spoke to that other person still obscured in the porch corner. "Aren't you going to come out?"

King Merrick's pulse quickened. An air of suppressed excitement was about him. A chair capsized and a man's muttered anger reached him, familiar yet unrecognizable. The next moment Dusty Tremaine appeared beside the girl. Dusty was tremendously sober. He looked once at King, seeming uneasy, and then switched his attention to Lolita. "I better be going."

27

"Why, you old horse thief," grunted King, relaxing. "Tryin' to steal my girl. Why didn't you say where you was goin' at supper time?"

"Oh, I reckon I was in a hurry," replied Dusty, still unsmiling. King caught some signal passing between the two. And though he was no hand at drawing motives out of peoples' eyes, the glow of pleasure deserted him. A man and a girl had to understand each other well to exchange unspoken thoughts like that. Dusty moved behind King and into the yard. "See you later," said he.

"Yeah," agreed King.

An interval of silence. Saddle leather creaked. "I was meanin' Lolita," added Dusty. His horse drummed away through the yard, bound in the direction of Five Echo.

King chuckled. "There's solid friendship. Dusty deserts a blamed nice place for his old friend."

Lolita said nothing. King stepped around her until he had his back to the light and he swung her gently until her features were clear and distinct to him. The hand dropped. "I sort of been waiting the time I could see you like this," said he, humbly. "I sent you some letters from Rawlins. Guess you never got them."

Her left hand rose and touched his arm.

Perhaps it was deliberately meant, perhaps it was the easiest way to soften a blow. King never knew. But he saw that his ring was not on her finger.

"I won't lie to you, King," she replied, still searching his face. It was very queer to him — the way she looked into his eyes and seemed to sound his heart. There was no middle ground with Lolita. Either she was gay and exuberant or she flung herself to the other extreme. Now she was somber, one small wrinkle furrowing between her black eyes. "I got your letters but — but — well, I knew I'd see you soon."

"Yeah, sure," muttered King. He drew a breath and reached for his cigarette papers. "Let's go over and sit in the corner. I'm sort of weary."

"No — I'd rather stand here," she said. "And see you. What have you done, King? Dusty and I thought you wouldn't come tonight, having ridden so far all day."

She was always frank, she never deceived. King raised his shoulders and dropped them, of a sudden feeling very tired. The news he carried seemed less worth giving now, less important. "Went to the land office outside and tied up a parcel of that government range south of Five Echo. It's mine." Then, slowly, amending the sentence. "It's ours."

"In Brierly country?" she demanded, suddenly interested.

"It's only been theirs because nobody wanted to raise a ruckus," said he. "Some folks thought they owned it. They don't. They just occupy open entry land. Too blamed lazy or too sure of themselves to file on it. I signed for a nice chunk of territory along the Middle Draw."

"The Middle Draw! King, all their trails run across the Middle Draw. They'll fight!"

"Their privilege," said King.

Lolita shook her head. "They will fight. You'll be a target, day or night. You can't watch all the time. Sooner or later they'll kill you. Oh, King, why did you pick that part of the country?"

King drew a breath. "To hold up my end of the bargain, Lolita."

Her head turned half away from him, she looked far into the shadows, and her words came back muffled and halting. "King, don't you see yet?"

"I'm a plain fellow, Lolita. I never was much good at guessin'."

"Oh, I think you see! Doesn't it mean something to you that Dusty was here tonight?"

He had no answer. All that for which he

had labored and all that for which he had so buoyantly hoped now lay in the dust. He had no answer for that. And turning she saw him look down at her hair with the expression of a man who wanted a last glance at something infinitely dear to him about to pass away.

"Dusty," he answered, very quietly, "is my friend. And he's a fine man. I couldn't expect you to get a better one."

Her hand brushed him and dropped into his coat pocket. She was giving him back the ring. "You were away all winter, King. And Dusty was here. It's better to find out now than afterwards. I know my faults, and I couldn't be a wife to make the best of a bad bargain. No, I don't mean that about you! You are all that Dusty is not and never can be. I'd always be safe and secure and taken care of with you. I'm not sure about Dusty. But — Dusty — "

"Yeah," drawled King. The crickets were sounding through the night. Sage smell trembled like incense in the air. Lolita's body swayed a little toward him. He never had seen her so beautiful, so vivid. And he was but a slow, plodding kind of man. It would have been the mating of a plow horse and a thorough-bred. "Yeah. But you love Dusty. I'm wishin' you luck. I reckon I had better be going."

She was still on the porch when he sat in the saddle. But, turning down the lane, he heard her crying, "King, wait a moment!" He sank his spurs, the horse raced onward toward Five Echo. And Lolita's last call chimed like a distant bell. "King!"

Why wait? What more was there to be said? It was over with him, and that phrase rhymed with the hoof beats and went through his brain again and again. It was over with him. What was Dusty ashamed about, why hadn't Dusty stayed to see it out? These things hurt — they hurt like hell! What was to be, was to be. Dusty should have stuck and fought his own battle instead of making Lolita do it. She was worth fighting for — even worth breaking up the deepest friendship. He, King Merrick, would have remained on that porch and faced the world if it had been his victory. Dusty hated to hurt people, so he had gone away. Now he had to find Dusty and go through the whole thing again — tell Dusty it was all right and that the best man won.

He raced onward. The stars were very dim, all sounds came to him from a distance. Turmoil boiled within, boiling up and spewing out the hopes he had nourished. All down the mile trail to Five Echo he left his dreams. The chapter was ended. For him it was utterly, irrevocably finished.

So he came into Five Echo and dismounted by the saloon, a familiar, stocky and dependable figure of a man that the valley was always glad to see. And there was nothing about him to mark a change, save that he carried himself a little straighter and his features were set in tighter lines.

Before he entered the saloon he knew that the Brierly clan was in town. Roosting on the saloon porch was a shoddy lump of a man known only as Silas. Silas was a nondescript hanger-on. But wherever the Brierlys were, Silas could always be found.

Chapter Three

Nobody knew a great deal about Silas. He had been in the valley twelve years, perhaps more; and as long as the valley's memory extended he had always been the same shiftless, slack figure. Nobody knew his last name, nobody cared. A dog on the street received as much attention as he was given. Even the Brierlys, with whom he lived and rode, treated him like an inferior animal. Silas never appeared to care. But Silas owned a pair of sharp, bird-like eyes that gleamed brilliantly within the casing of his puffy, pitted face. And the Brierlys always had need for such eyes.

When King Merrick stepped to the porch Silas met him with a distinct freshening of interest and his boots curled beneath his body as if he wanted to move away. His chin ducked. " 'Lo, Mister Merrick."

"Hello, Silas. Still on the job?"

"Whut job?"

"Well, the job of just sittin'," replied King. "And maybe seein' what folks aim to do."

"Yuh never saw me work," parried Silas, baring his teeth for what was meant as a grin. "I don't hafta work. I'm a provided man, Mister Merrick."

"Gettin' fat on it, too," observed King.

Silas bowed significantly, lowering his voice. "I found a root up in the hills, Mister Merrick. It's the nutriment o' the Lord. All the Lord's chil'ren git fat on it."

King turned to the saloon doors. The valley had a notion that Silas was simple. The man certainly gave out that impression. King wondered if he was, and was inclined to doubt it. King shoved the doors before him to find a subdued group of men idling in the chairs and along the wall, watching a half-dozen Brierlys drink at the bar. These Brierlys were all the same, the whole pack of them — brothers, sons and cousins — tall, loose-jointed fellows, black jowled and deep of eye socket. They had never been made for humor. The grace of friendliness or the smooth word was not in them. Only about half the clan was here tonight, but Rolf Brierly stood in the center of the group, a self-sure, commanding figure. King's attention went directly to him and this Brierly, hearing the doors swing, turned. He shoved his glass away which was a signal for the rest to follow suit.

"Evenin', Merrick. Back for spring work?"

"That's about it, Rolf," said King, grinning at his other friends in the room. His would have been a boisterous welcome except for the damping presence of the clan.

Rolf Brierly dismissed the whole group of bystanders with a single indifferent turn of his head. He bowed at King. "Have a drink with me."

"Believe I will, Rolf. What've you been doin' for exercise durin' the winter?"

Rolf grinned and pinched his lean jaw. "Too cold to do anything, Merrick. Heard yuh took some considerable trip outside. I'll be envyin' yuh on that. I get sorter cramped with these hills and I'd like to have a little look around. But, sho', if I left my folks alone they'd cook up a mess of trouble in a minute."

"Which don't seem a charitable opinion of your own kinfolk," mused King, lifting his glass.

Rolf Brierly matched the move. "The gent that said charity begins at home didn't much know human nature, Merrick. A fambly livin' elbow to elbow ain't got any room for charity. All Brierlys are good hard men. But they're dumb. I'm the only one in three generations

36

with enough imagination to wish for a look beyont the ridges. Brierlys have got too much bone and muscle. I'd trade any three of the pack for a man who could play the fiddle. Here's how."

They drank and observed an appropriate silence following. These two were on opposite sides of the fence. By every standard of right and wrong as well as of sentiment they belonged to opposite camps. And each was clear sighted enough to know a day might come in which they would match wit and gun. Even so, they shared a respect. A healthy respect.

In some ways they were quite similar. Both of them were of that type to brush away words and come bluntly to the issue. They were both leaders; Rolf a leader through sheer force, King Merrick a leader through the valley's plain knowledge of his ability to command a difficulty. Each possessed the troublesome power of looking beyond faults and circumstances to see the good that existed in the opposing man. And perhaps, away down deep in the nature of these two, some small amount of sympathy and admiration existed. King Merrick, so mild and self-effacing, had never turned a hand to gain the popular approval that was his in so full a measure. His path had been peaceful and humdrum, nor had he ever strayed outside the law. It was otherwise with the great, rawboned Brierly. He had brushed all obstacles aside, the commandments were flimsy barriers he obeyed or disobeyed as the spirit moved him. Now he stood as the ruler of a little world both uncertain and monotonous.

"Maybe," suggested King, "you need a little bad news for a tonic."

Brierly looked to the four corners of the room as if to ask, where would it come from among these weaklings? King shifted his weight.

"I reckon I'm sorry to say it," said King, genuinely regretful, "but I'll have to furnish the bad news, Rolf. I need some room to spread out in. So I've filed on a section of government land in the Middle draw. Steppin' on your toes some, but I need it."

It was a full challenge to the power of the Brierlys, nor would any of them fail to regard it as such. Yet King Merrick, closely watching the clan leader, saw nothing but the minutest steadying of face muscles to mark the change.

"Have another drink," suggested Rolf.

"One's ample," declined King. "I'm obliged for the hospitality."

"Yuh missed a tough winter here," mused

Brierly. "But Spring's early at that. Somethin' mighty powerful about sap runnin' time ain't they, Merrick? I wish I could ride sometime with a man like you, which could see what I see at sunup an' sundown. This pack o' long, lean, hungry houn's eat too much meat. They don't see nothin'. Smoke in the hills pritty soon. We'll all be a year older. Ever git started on that train o' figgerin', Merrick?"

"It don't lead anywhere," drawled King. "When a man reaches that pass he's just talkin' to make echoes."

"I guess," murmured Brierly, lolling against the bar. The room was dead still. Moment by moment Rolf built up a suspense that drummed against man's nerves. Merrick had laid down a challenge sure to be accepted. Yet so casually did Rolf Brierly dwell upon it that those in the room were for a little while taken unawares. "About yore filin' — figger to string fences pritty soon, uh?"

"Soon's I get some spare time beyond roundup," was Merrick's mild answer. "One strand of barb-wire will have to do this year."

"Middle Draw is nice country," sleepily observed Brierly. He swept the room again, marking the effect of his words. A flicker of ironic amusement rose to his eyes. But when he returned his glance to Merrick that amusement was displaced by regret. "Always wondered why somebody didn't try to file it before."

"Folks never wanted it bad enough I'd calculate," King replied, patently weary from his long day's activity.

"You want it pritty bad, uh?"

"Filed on it."

Brierly shook his head. "Sorter wish you'd filed on Thumb or Little Finger instead. It's campin' pritty close to our front door."

"Figured there might be some little difficulty," said King, looking up. Brierly studied him a long, long moment. His big shoulders rose.

"I'll hate to do it, Merrick," he muttered.

"Fair and open?" asked King, straightening.

"As for myself, that goes. But I told yuh already this pack o' mine ain't got no imagination. I can't keep tally on twelve, fifteen dumb brutes."

"Do the best you can and so will I," said King. He turned toward the door. Once during the parley he had seen Dusty Tremaine look in and duck back again. King left the saloon, and not until he was gone did the whole significance of that short interview between Brierly and Merrick fall upon the bystanders. One had challenged, the other accepted; neither had raised his voice above the pitch of moderation.

Dusty Tremaine kept to the shadows. King saw him standing very still, as if hoping to avoid a meeting, but he crossed over and touched Dusty on the shoulder. "It's all right, Dusty," King said. "Never run away from something you've got to face. Never lay down an ace full without bettin' it. Lord bless you, old-timer!"

"King, I'd rather take a lickin' — " Dusty stammered.

Merrick interrupted with a half angry vehemence. "You dam' fool, don't you know what you've won? Get on your horse and go back to Bench S!"

Dusty choked and crowded a phrase through the darkness. "Still friends, King? Listen, I fought this thing out, but it didn't do no good — "

"Still friends," muttered King. "Go back to Bench S." He dropped off the porch and put the shadows between himself and Dusty. They would still be friends, yet they would never be the same friends. That was wisdom as old as life.

In a dark spot along the street King tarried. Dusty hadn't taken his advice about going back to Bench S. His partner was talking softly and rapidly with somebody beyond

41

the saloon lights. The swinging doors opened and a Brierly came out. More phrases, sharper and higher. A horseman flung himself north along the valley road but it wasn't Dusty Tremaine.

It lacked a half hour of nine. King Merrick was dead tired, tired enough to sleep on his feet. Directly in front beamed the invitation of N. Porterfield's Valley Restaurant. Since N. Porterfield had arrived in Five Echo one year ago and established a restaurant, there had always been a light shining out of the window from dusk till dawn. After regular hours any passing rider might enter and help himself of the coffee pot warming on the kitchen stove.

King entered and sat up to the counter. N. Porterfield's head was bent over a letter. It rose slowly, then the letter was forgotten and N. Porterfield came quickly to the counter with a rare, warm smile and a welcome that went straight through him.

"King — I'm glad to see you back!"

N. Porterfield was a girl with copper-colored hair and hazel eyes. An upstanding girl with a grave and finely thoughtful countenance that seldom was relaxed from a hint of sadness. Yet when, as now, the gravity was broken there was a light irresistibly attractive. To the valley she was another mystery. A dozen men wanted to marry her and she was of marriageable age. Yet she refused all offers, which caused the valley to shake its head over the sad waste of family possibilities.

He took her hand, smiling back. "Expected I'd return to find you with a partner."

"What kind of a partner, King?"

"The kind the parson gives you for life, Nancy."

She drew back a little, the better to watch his face. Her lips were pursed; amusement lay in the upturned corners of her mouth. Many men had matched wits with Nancy Porterfield on this subject. "Perhaps nobody wants me, King."

"Shucks, there's dozens of 'em straining on the leash."

"We-ell, maybe I've been waiting for a particular man," she said.

That aroused his interest. "Now that's interestin'. Who might he be? A fellow hasn't got any right to be particular with a girl like you. Who's the rascal?"

And Nancy, knowing King's bashfulness, looked directly at him, very sober. "Maybe it's you."

He squirmed in the chair, only the deep tan of his face concealing what otherwise would have been a flush. Nancy turned away, color rising to her own cheeks. She had used this answer on many a puncher, routing them easily. But the moment she said it to King embarrassment overtook her. "Coffee?" she asked meekly.

"Strong," he said. "Lots of it, and a piece of pie. Nancy, I've tried a hundred restaurants this winter but I can't find any pie like yours."

"Another good point about me, King," the girl smiled. "I offer it for your consideration. King, I *am* glad to see you back. There's been such an uneasy feeling around us all winter. Like something suspended and ready to drop."

She placed coffee and pie before him and cupped her chin in her hand. King seemed uninterested at the news but the girl knew that to be only the habitual poker expression of the range man absorbing important facts. "Well," said he, "from the mud hereabouts it looks as if old Jupe might be on the verge o' droppin' his sprinklin' can. Nancy, I wish I could eat this pie three times a day."

"Is that a proposal, Mister Merrick?" she came right back.

"You leave me alone young lady. What's the matter with the valley?"

"So you change the subject to protect yourself," she jeered. Soberness swiftly followed.

"I wish I knew what the exact trouble was. But I feel it. Let me tell you something, King. I have heard more of the valley men grumbling than ever before, and rolling their eyes toward the five draws. Many a night I've heard riders go past, traveling fast. And what makes the Brierlys come down out of their stronghold so much recently? They used to keep strictly to themselves."

"That all?"

"Isn't it enough?" she demanded.

"If there's a fire there's got to be something that makes it burn," he said. "In the simple language of a homely gent — beef."

"Well, I have never heard anybody openly accuse the Brierlys of that," she mused aloud.

"And you won't, either, unless they take more than their share. Maybe you don't exactly catch on to the sort of politics we believe in hereabouts. None of us is goin' to accuse a Brierly of rustlin'. No Brierly would ever deny rustlin' if accused. We know they do it — they know we know they do it. But the consensus of opinion around here is that so long's they are plumb moderate with their irons and don't pick on any one brand for more than a few cows and calves it's cheaper to let 'em get away with it than to blast 'em out of their castle. I wouldn't have to explain this except that you've only been here a year or so and it takes longer than that to understand our left-handed view point."

"So you let them get away with outright stealing. Oh, King, that doesn't sound like *you.*"

"Who am I?" was his astonished question.

"You're a man," she retorted. "And one little word from you would bring this whole valley together."

"You've got me way over estimated, Nancy. Ten years ago we could have stopped it with no great trouble. Now they sort of regard it as a right to levy their tax. It don't hurt us any, so long as they pick a critter here and another there."

"It isn't right!" she insisted.

He shrugged his shoulders. "I know it. But it's practical." He leaned forward, and the girl saw for the first time a worn look about his eyes. "Remember, Nancy, when the valley starts to clean the Brierlys out of here somebody dies. That's why I say it's practical to let 'em alone while they're moderate. If they get overweaning that's a different story. But I don't like to see men die."

The door opened and Pack MacGabriel thrust his head through, looking beside and above King but never directly at him. "Excuse me. Thought I'd find one of the boys here." And he disappeared. King casually paid his bill and slid from the stool, rolling a cigarette. He took his time doing it, head thoughtfully bowed. The girl observed the dexterity of his fingers, calloused and thick as they were; and she noted again as she had many times before, the blunt honesty of his features and the lurking kindliness around his mouth and eyes. He was tired beyond a physical weariness. She saw that too.

He drew a breath of smoke and nodded toward the street. "I guess I'm progressin' in the direction of old age. This wild night life don't suit me any more. Better travel."

She leaned over the counter. "King — maybe we — I know more of your affairs than you think. Oh, King, I'm sorry!"

He understood. Passing out, he looked back a moment, gray and grim. "Thanks a heap. But the cards can't favor everybody, Nancy."

"They ought to favor *you!*" said she, voice striking sharply on the words. He ducked his head again and closed the door. He paused against the wall, looking to either direction, listening. Then he crossed the street and cruised slowly along the walk to the hotel. The saloon porch directly opposite appeared deserted. King missed the familiar shadow that was Silas. But the Brierlys still were inside drinking.

Strolling into the hotel King nodded at the clerk and walked upstairs and down the hall to a room; entered without knocking and faced seven cattlemen whose combined range covered approximately eighty percent of the valley's extent. He knew them all intimately — MacGabriel, Hedges, the elder Tape and the younger Tape, Pinchot, Spring, and Dad Labadie. He ran the roll, calling their names and shaking hands, and observing the set gravity of each. Nobody slapped him familiarly on the back, nobody joked about his adventures outside though on almost any other occasion they would have done so. King sat in a chair, waiting.

Pack MacGabriel cleared his throat. "King, you got a chore to do. We will warn you it is a serious one. It means trouble, maybe ambush. That, however, ain't the worst of it. There may come a time when you'll have to take a harder blow than anything in the line of lead. Accept it?"

"Yeah."

It seemed to King they could never have doubted his willingness. Yet he saw relief and some other significant expression relay from owner to owner. MacGabriel appeared to find it difficult to carry on from his blunt beginning. "We waited till you got back. Nobody else can do this chore like you. Oh, they's plenty of hot young fellows, plenty of boys with guts and plenty with ability on the draw. But it's been our opinion some long time that when you went out to do something it got done, no matter how slow you traveled. Yore as dependable, by Gollus, as the solar system."

"Any flowers go with that?" asked King, smiling with embarrassment. "Or how about ten dollars more a month in the old pay check?"

"I'm payin' you more'n yore worth now," grumbled MacGabriel. "I wouldn't be swellin' yore head with these big words only we want to impress the nature o' this affair on yuh. And to say in short that all seven of us, with all the money we got and all the men and guns and horses we got, as well as all the time we got, is behind you. It's yores to call on. The point is, King, the Brierlys have gone into rustlin' wholesale. And we mean to stop it."

"It had to come someday," muttered King.

"Perhaps so," MacGabriel went on. "Well, showdown has got to come likewise. Yore job is to go out and get the evidence, the clear and plain evidence. Enough of it to convince any jury in the world. More than enough to convince a jury, because in the long run this won't mebbe ever get as far as a jury. It depends on you. And we will say further that though you are to look for Brierlys in this rustlin', you will have to look for some one hand or mebbe more than one hand who is workin' on the payroll of somebody in this room!"

King threw back his head. "A Judas wearin' chaps? What makes you figger so, Pack?"

"They couldn't possibly work so slick and quiet without somebody from inside helpin' 'em," the rancher explained. "You got to find out. You got to see the Brierlys rustle with yore own eyes, you got to run yore own fingers over blotched brands, you got to discover the exact trail they take. More than that, you got to find this dam' traitor. You will be the only witness and yore testimony is all we want. On said testimony we aim to crucify the Brierlys and whatever man who is eatin' our bread and stealin' our stock."

King stirred in the chair. "One man's judgment is pritty small to bank on in a case like this, Pack."

"It's too big an order for anybody in the valley but you," said the rancher. "More than one man would gum the machinery, warn off the game. Anyhow there ain't another fellow on hand able enough to trail with you. So it's one man's word and yore elected, King, because yore honest to the bone."

"It sounds like grief to me," murmured King.

MacGabriel wasn't finished yet. He scanned the other ranchers for support before continuing. "We're wishin' you'd stand up, King."

Merrick did so. MacGabriel cleared his throat. "We are askin' that you'll raise yore right hand and swear on yore honor you will see this job through to the bitter end, no matter what happens, no matter how it hurts, no matter what names go down in the mire; and that you will speak what you have discovered and all that you have discovered."

"I will," King said, raising his arm.

In the lull following he rolled a cigarette, conscious that these seven hard-headed men were raking him to the very core for sign of weakness. "What makes you think it's goin' to jolt somebody so doggone hard?" he wanted to know.

"Because," replied Pack and considered that a sufficient answer. "In the mornin' you'll ride out towards Section Line wash with the boys. When yuh go into the brush, just keep right on. It's yore job then. I'm finished."

King pulled down his hat and departed. A yard or so from the hotel he drifted to the deepest shadows and waited while the ranch owners casually emerged from their meeting and separately departed from the town. A stray valley man left the saloon and likewise rode out. Nothing else moved on the street. The horses of the Brierlys were yet waiting by the saloon rack but he could find nothing of the inevitable harbinger of their presence — Silas. Presently he crossed, got his own pony, and turned him toward the Music Box.

As King passed Nancy Porterfield's restaurant he saw her through the window bent over the counter talking with animation to Rolf Brierly. It strangely upset all of King's ideas about her and left a slight uneasiness in him though he couldn't understand why. The roadside gloom enveloped him.

Within two minutes of his passing Silas ducked around the hotel and sprang into the saloon. Immediately thereafter a Brierly came out and spurred from town in the general direction King Merrick had taken but swinging off the road at a wide angle.

King jogged homeward, mind laden with the events of the evening. Tonight all that he had labored to achieve was in the dust and he was turned from peace to a manhunt. He never yet had raised his gun at a man. Yet in the space of ten minutes he had been appointed to destroy.

He was at the four mile post from town. His horse stepped aside in the road, shying. A shadow grew out of a fence. A shot shattered the night's silence. The point of flame centered King's vision. Low in the saddle and unhurt he sent his bullets at a fugitive racing away. King put his horse to the fence, jumped and followed. Another shot missed him. And the rider vanished toward the bench. King was too tired to follow. This was the opening of a hard fight, the announcement of the Brierlys that he knew his future part. So he set the pony to a lope and went down the Music Box side path.

Chapter Four

The crew of the Music Box was away from the home quarters by break of day, lining out across the meadows where the fox swirled and eddied against the passage of their horses. The hint of another fair, hot morning lay above them, striving against the damp and crisp chill of a winter not quite gone. Two by two they rode through the wet grass, drummed over a bridge and on into the sage. King Merrick and Dusty Tremaine went side by side, talking beef as if nothing had passed between their long established friendship.

Dusty was a volatile man, easy to sway and swiftly reacting to the mood of the land. His bold and handsome face raked the foregound. A cigarette drooped between his full and smiling lips. Eagerness to be up and doing glimmered in his hazel eyes. Nothing could damp the love of excitement in this man. The fact that he had put one disagreeable scene behind him — the interview with King of the previous night — seemed only to throw his gay spirit the higher. He lived from one rebound of restlessness to another; and whatever was behind Dusty Tremaine was closed and forgotten.

One hour later the thinning fog showed them the rolling sides of Section Line wash running down from the ridge. A corral, partly filled with steer stuff cut out from the herd for spring market, sprawled here. Directly behind began the pine scattered bench, marked by cattle trails and sharp ravines lying dark and silent in the morning's mists. The Music Box outfit halted and looked to King Merrick.

"What's the spread?" asked Slim Martis.

"You boys covered the territory towards Circle J yesterday. This mornin' we'd better go straight up into the buck brush. Two head up as far as the Bald Knob and come back. Two more take from Bald Knob to the first line cabin. Third set from the line cabin to Eagle Pass. Rest string out on the bench and pick up what's hazed down. That's plenty of work for today. You're still proddin' the outfit, Dusty. I won't be around."

"Where you goin'?" asked Dusty.

Slim Martis was rolling a cigarette. One

sharp glance crossed from himself to King Merrick. King debated with his conscience a moment. Slim knew more of the business ahead of him than the rest of the crew. Stoney suspected something but didn't know a great deal. The rest of the crew, King believed, was ignorant of his mission. As for Dusty, he wasn't sure. Dusty's eyes were boring curiously into him.

"I'm makin' a round of our range," said King. "Want to see how everything lies for the year. Think maybe some of our spread is over on range, and I figger a lot of stuff is on ours. Won't be back till late. Hop to."

He rode away while the rest of the outfit split and went on their appointed circles. Spurs and bridle chains tinkled in the cold air. A shout from Dusty Tremaine echoed musically; then King was in the pines, following a trail slanting sharply upward. A cow bawled somewhere in the thicket. The horse beneath him bunched his muscles for the climb. When the sun broke through King stood on the backbone of the ridge, sweeping the green and glistening land below. A number of trails wound before him. He took that one going directly south toward the higher and more rugged country of the five draws.

Though King had been pledged to secrecy

regarding his present job, he felt embarrassed at concealing it from Dusty — deliberately misleading Dusty. They had shared everything over so long a period that it seemed a little like treachery not to do so now. He shook his head regretfully.

"The old times are gone. What's the use of thinking different?"

He arrived at a burn and again paused. Eastward beyond this area of charred snags and blackened earth the ridge began to grow rougher, its backbone broken by peaks and deep draws. King studied the country between half closed lids. "The Brierlys are brash people. It's an even bet they drive all rustled critters direct into the Five Draws. Up till now they've had no particular necessity of deception. By the Lord, I wish it was somebody else on this manhunt. I don't particularly like to fight."

King proceeded due south on the main ridge trail for a good two hours, traveling leisurely, reading the stray signs of the earth. Away down in the valley he saw a single wisp of smoke and a blur of moving figures. That was Spring's outfit working their calves over. The trail presently began to curve in and slope a little down hill, constricting the valley.

A small excitement pervaded King Merrick. He spoke urgently to the plodding horse and the gait quickened. Down the twisting path they picked their way. Level ground met them and across this they went. With equal suddenness the terrain swooped upward into the dark and deceptive folds of the Five Draws. King Merrick reined in, facing the narrow runway of the Middle Draw. Up that lonely pathway a distance of three or four miles was the log castle of the Brierlys. Along this draw they rode on their forays to Five Echo. It was land they claimed by right of power. Yet it was not theirs legally. King Merrick stood in the very heart of the section he had filed on this winter while outside.

King rolled a cigarette, surveying the trees with a tight grin. It was his land — the first piece of land he had ever laid claim to. Water and grass and pine were his even though the pounding hoofs of the Brierlys had laid a wide beaten track across it. Fight — sure they'd fight to keep that track open. It was the main gateway to their mountain retreat. Well, he would fight back. It was his.

"Southwest corner of this section should be beyond the creek," he murmured. "Let's see if we can find the surveyor's mark." The pony, obedient to the rein pressure, crossed the trail and pressed through the overhanging boughs. A creek sprang out of the hills, deep and turbulent. Upward a matter of fifty yards a long bridge crossed the water. As King swung to reach the bridge his eyes caught the brightness of a woman's dress beside a tree. She heard the sound of his advance and turned out of the shelter. Nancy Porterfield's grave face, drawn tight with expectancy, looked up to him.

"King!" she exclaimed.

"You're a long ways from home, lady," replied King, lifting his hat.

She had heard him coming and had thought it someone else. That was plain. The troubled expression left her eyes for the moment, her hands dropped away from her breast. King stepped to the ground, and saw that she had been crying. He turned his head, not wanting to break in on her secret, and rolled a cigarette, immensely concerned. She had always been so strong and serene and self-reliant that this sign of weakness came as a distinct surprise. Her slow, subdued question drew his attention back.

"What are you doing away over here, King?" she asked.

"Lookin' over a piece of my land," he replied.

"Your land, King?"

"I filed on this durin' the winter."

"Here — along the Middle Draw? Why King, they — they won't let you!"

"Speakin' of the Brierlys?" he countered. Within the four walls of the restaurant she had always appeared tall and sure. Out here she was but a slender, auburn-haired woman with tight fists and gray worried eyes that seemed to contain a mute appeal. "Don't let that name trouble you too much, Nancy. It's been built up by a lot of hocus-pocus."

"King, don't talk so confidently. Don't ride so openly through these trees. Just one bullet — and the Brierlys are hard men."

"Hold on here," said he. "Ain't you got troubles enough without assumin' mine? I'm not that particular chap you was speakin' about."

She shook her head. "I do worry, nevertheless."

"Why?"

She looked into the swift waters of the creek. King noticed for the first time the gentleness and the quiet beauty of her rounding features. This aspect of Nancy Porterfield was new to him, for in the restaurant she always wore a confidence to ward off the persiflage of the ranch hands. And still avoiding his eyes she answered him. "Oh, because I'm a woman, I guess."

He studied the tip of his cigarette. "You're in trouble. It's none of my business but maybe it'd help to share it. You shoulder my trouble. I'll shoulder yours."

It touched her visibly. She swung around and put a hand to his arm. "King, I wish I could!"

"Why not then?" he went on.

"Because."

He smiled. "Full, illuminatin', comprehensive and complete. Nancy, you sure are a woman."

"King, you are the one man I would want to see me as a woman."

He studied that at length, so soberly that a trace of color came to her cheeks and she interrupted. "Don't try to figure it out. Do me a favor."

"Done."

"Go away and leave me here. I — I am to meet somebody."

She wouldn't look directly at him. King got into the saddle and crossed the bridge and without further word went through the trees and lost sight of her. His own business carried him three full miles away from the spot but the farther he traveled the more the puzzle grew. What could she be doing up here, why did she have to meet with anybody so far from Five Echo? Maybe it was none of his business. And again, maybe she needed help. That one small interview had wholly changed the picture of Nancy Porterfield for him. She had always been distant. Now she was human and desirable, and in trouble. He shook his head and put this sort of thinking resolutely behind him. He had come to the far point of his day's journey and needed all his wits.

King stood beside another small creek breaking down the bottom of another dark runway from the hills, the last such runway to be crossed on the way to the west ridge of the valley. Turning the horse, King started back, picking a path somewhat deeper in the rugged reaches of the hills, eyes roving the earth for sign.

On his left was the valley, narrowing like a man's wrist; to his right five fissures cleft the upthrusting terrain, like fingers extending from that wrist and tapering outward in much the same manner. The earliest settlers of the country recognized the analogy and named the draws accordingly, Thumb, Forefinger, Middle, Ring and Little Finger Draw. The valley and the ridges east and west were settled and occupied range land. But where the draws began and as far as they extended southward and upward into this difficult and forbidding area of pine peaks and brush woven glens the Brierlys held control. King Merrick began his hunt with this fact in mind. If cattle tracks crossed the imaginary line from valley to Brierly soil they only did so because they had been driven over by the clan on a rustling foray.

Therefore King went methodically about his job, traversing the mouth of the clan's territory at the narrowest point. The Brierlys rustled, and were not particular in covering their tracks. They had been too long at rustling to be cautious. And they had a tremendous pride in their strength.

Noon found King back at the Middle Draw. Nancy was no longer there but King saw the downward mark of her horse, and he also saw the hoof prints of another animal leading from higher up the trail. He might have looked closer and found where a man's boots had walked beside Nancy's smaller shoe, yet he pressed forward, shaking his head at the impulse. "It's her affair. Why should I be sneakin' around and spyin' her business?"

King found cattle tracks along Ring Draw that interested him. He plunged deeper into the hills, ascending that draw until he had fully satisfied himself that these tracks were ancient history. He was after more recent rustling. So he retraced his way and passed along a thin, secretive path for better than a mile. At Little Finger Draw he forded a yard-wide creek, started to drag the land between this creek and the bench, and rode directly upon the fresh sign for which he patiently quested. A herd of twenty or more cattle had been driven into Brierly territory no longer than two nights ago.

Within a quarter of an hour's criss-crossing of those tracks King discovered something else. The Brierlys had not brought them directly from the valley but from some high point in the eastern ridge. The trail turned into Little Finger from a sharp angle. King sat on his horse and smoked a long cigarette, debating whether to follow up the draw or cruise back and discover the origin of the rustled stuff. He decided on the latter course. The next link in the chain was not to find out where the Brierlys hid their stolen beef, but to locate that exact spot where the Brierlys received the stock from the traitor in the valley.

"Always supposin' Pack MacGabriel's belief as to the existence of said traitor bein' true," mused King. "I ain't so sure. A Brierly is old enough and Indian enough to find and snake out his own beef. Why should they split with a valley hand, or tip off their game to somebody not in the clan? Still, it might be so. Anyhow we'll augur along the back trail a little bit."

He set the pony in motion with the mark of the cattle for a plain compass point. Sometimes he had a view of the trail for fifty yards ahead; then the trees cramped down and he kept his eyes directly before the pony's head. Always that trail angled higher on the ridge and a little to the north, taking a roundabout way toward some point around the burn King had earlier skirted. The afternoon grew on. King rolled another cigarette and checked his horse a moment. And at exactly that moment he knew he was being followed.

There was no particular reason for knowing, no tangible sight or sound or smell King could lay his senses against. Nevertheless the warning ran up and down his back and stiffened him in the saddle for the instant like a piece of marble. He checked the impulse to reach for his gun and he denied the desire to turn and cover his rear. He spoke gently to the horse and laid a rein against its neck. The path of the cattle bellied deeper into the pines. King turned off and with a leisureliness that screwed up his nerves, paced into the open. He counted the yards to himself. Beyond good revolver range he breathed a tremendous sigh. The main path up to the backbone of the ridge lay in front and he took it, winding with it, around this tree and that. And when a good two hundred yards of open space intervened he looked quite casually back; and saw nothing at all in the green thicket.

It made no difference. The warning was clear and distinct. King quickened his pace. Now and then as the increasing altitude allowed him wider vision he swept his wake, never at any time catching sight of a moving creature. Presently he came to the fringe of the burn. Beyond was heavy timber. He reached the timber and set the horse to a stiff gallop for some fifty yards. Then with the same suddenness, he checked the horse, forced it deep in the trees and left it there; himself returning to the edge of the path and squatting behind a dead stump.

It never occurred to him his mind might have played him a trick. These warnings rarely came to him. When they did he obeyed them implicitly. Therefore he was not surprised to hear a rhythmic padding of feet strike down between the trees perhaps twenty minutes later. He drew his gun and tilted the muzzle. Silas, the camp follower of the Brierlys, came to sight, passed him within arm's length and scuttled on out of view.

The man's face was set like that of a hound and his eyes had been as bright as diamonds.

"He ain't so all-fired crazy," muttered King. "Nothing seems to get past him. How long has he been on my heels? And what am I goin' to do about it? There's a potent question for an amateur range inspector. I ought to have my book of rules along. 'Situation One Hundred and Eleven: What to do when a sawed-off human scarecrow turns mountain beagle and sets down to pursue.' Dam' the man."

The sound of Silas returning, preceded him through the lane of trees. He repassed King with the same shambling trot and was lost around the bend. King rose and followed, keeping well within reach of concealment. Before he quite came to the end of the stand of pines he had sight of Silas wandering across the burn. In a little while the man stopped and dropped flat to the charred earth. King waited patiently. By and by Silas rose, looked all about him and reached to his pocket. He drew out a bit of cloth and jammed it in the crack of a black snag. Once more he swept his surroundings with a series of birdlike twists of his head and then bent into the monotonous dog trot, darting across the burn. He struck the main trail back to Brierly country and disappeared below the slope.

"A signal for who?" King asked himself.

He returned to his horse and led it out of the thicket, still musing over the question. "Well, a signal for somebody. Is it or ain't it significant that said flag is right on the trail leadin' over to that mess of pockets east of the ridge back? King, you go home, eat a bite and return here about dark."

He climbed up and obeyed the injunction. The sun flamed like a cauldron of fire, sank below the western line. It was beyond seven when he reached the ranch house. The boys already had eaten. King took a solitary snack and sat on the bunkhouse steps, smoking. Dusty Tremaine came out, dressed in his gaudy calling clothes.

Chapter Five

Dusty leaned against the bunkhouse wall and grinned casually at King. "Yuh must've ridden all four corners of Music Box territory, old-timer. Yuh looked tired a heap. What's on yore chest?"

"A flannel shirt," said King, smiling back. "I see you're all painted up for a war dance. I'm makin' a suggestion — why not pitch a tent halfway between Music Box and Spring's place? You wouldn't nowise have to ride so far either way."

Dusty's grin widened at the suggestion. King stared at the ground. He was just talking to make echoes and it didn't come easy. He didn't want Dusty to see his eyes. He had beaten down the trail to Spring's place and now Dusty followed it while he, King Merrick, sat on the steps and struggled to be indifferent. It was a trail he wouldn't be taking again.

Dusty moved to the front of King and looked swiftly around the yard. The humor died from his wide mouth. He dropped a quiet warning. "Listen, King," Dusty said, "mebbe yuh don't know what's been pilin' up around the valley all winter. I ain't a hand to carry gossip. Most gossip is nothin' but lies. But don't you travel too deep in the draw country after dark."

"Why?"

"I'm just tellin' it," responded Dusty and walked away to the corrals. King watched him saddle and mount. As Dusty prepared to follow that familiar trail down the twilight King threw his cigarette far in front of him, murmuring "Good luck, kid."

Dusty's face came around, drawn to a sharp, almost startled expression. "Yeah," he grunted and spurred away.

King rose and went about getting a fresh pony for the night's journey.

When he rode across the yard, Pack Mac-Gabriel was on the porch. King circled toward his boss and tarried. "I reckon the Brierlys know my hole card, Pack," he said.

"Pretty hard to keep it secret," grumbled MacGabriel. "Didn't I tell you they was a leak in the valley? Any news?"

"Plenty of tracks. I'll have something to tell in the morning I think." King started away, halting to add another thought. "If I don't get back in a reasonable length of time you'd better get a posse and go along the ridge trail to Little Finger. Straight up Little Finger till you see what you see."

"I sort of hoped you'd give us some idea like that," Pack said. "We're set to ride on five minutes' notice. King, play it safe. I don't want a dead foreman."

King chuckled. "If it comes to flowers, Pack, I really prefer orchids."

"Orchids, you dam' idiot? It'd be just as cheap to use chip diamonds."

King rode away, firing this last shot: "Well, I've got to get my money out of this bankrupt spread somehow. Orchids, nothin' less, Pack."

King traveled arrow straight to the bench, up the rough folds to the ridge's backbone and silently along the main trail. To that point he had ridden rapidly. Afterwards he drew the horse to a walk. The compressing trees threw all sound far along the path. The click of an iron shoe against some small rock beat away like the echo of a rifle shot awaking King to a still greater caution. Horse and rider reached the edge of the burn and drew off the trail.

"That little flag was a signal for somebody to turn off," King mused. "I wonder if that somebody has been by yet? I reckon so, for that flag was meant to be seen by daylight. Question, do I wait or do I go on? If I wait I may be missing something over in those pockets. If I wait I may be here all night. Answer is, I go on."

He avoided the side trail weaving across the heart of the burn and kept it well to one edge. Afar he thought he saw a reflected glow and steered accordingly.

Into one depression King dipped and up to the tip on another and taller butte. King saw again the shuttering of a hidden fire reflected on the opposite face of some ravine. Very, very quietly he dropped from the saddle. He had heard the sound of cattle shuffling below him in the trough of the buttes.

"They didn't cross the burn," said King Merrick to himself. "They ain't headed on that kind of a course. Must've come around 'way east of the ridge trail. If so it's dam' close to bein' either our cows or Spring's."

The cattle were deep enough in the shadows of the ravine to be safely out of sight; thirty or forty feet below. King Merrick kept his place, not wanting to put himself against the skyline for discovery. The herd traveled around the base of the butte upon which he stood. Knowing what he did of the land's contour, King could guess at what approximate point they would fall into the extraordinarily broken area on eastward. Climbing up to the saddle he set a parallel course, left the butte and was lost in the black recesses beyond.

A quarter hour's wandering brought King to a blind end. He put the horse to a stiff grade, belly bands groaning under the stress. The grade leveled in front of a solitary juniper. Before him lay a bowl swirling with fog and shadow; and at one extreme corner a fire flickered brilliantly.

Men moved around the fire restlessly, all standing erect and faced westward. King judged that the sound of the advancing beef drew their attention. He himself was too far removed to catch the sound; nor could he distinguish any of the men revealed in the ruby glow. He thought he identified the tallest of the group as Rolf Brierly but the identification was too doubtful to hold under oath.

Dismounting, King slid warily down the long incline and came to rest behind a layer of volcanic rock. A newcomer appeared in the light, also on foot, and crouched at the flames, whereat the group gathered close around.

"That gent brought the stock by himself,"

opined King, trying to catch some distinguishing feature of the man. "I guess Pack's right. There's somebody inside the valley helpin' the Brierlys. And there that somebody stands. I got to slide closer."

King left the rock and slid head-first, knee and elbow. The parley broke up before he had gone ten yards. The newcomer strolled out of the light, waving his hand in a lazy semicircle. The rest of the group dissolved in the darkness, one man kicking the fire apart as he passed. King abandoned a part of his caution and rose upright, covering the slope in full strides. The scattered flames went wreathing in the wind. One man rode back and paused a moment. King heard him calling; then the fellow went away.

King approached to within a few yards and dropped on his haunches, barely outside the ring of light. The cattle were moving around that light, climbing southward into the recesses of the ridge. An hour and they would be cruising up Little Finger Draw. Still King kept his place, forever exploring the outer shadows. When that rider had returned to the camp spot he had called somebody's name. Who remained behind —

At the very edge of the fire King saw a pair of buckskin gloves, the kind worn by punchers in the valley. King got a firmer grip on himself and kept quiet. Maybe those gloves were bait. The Brierlys were a shrewd bunch. At least one of them had enough imagination to pull such a trick — the reckless Rolf.

All sound of the cattle died, sucked into the vast vault. King was losing time here. His place was right behind that rustling outfit. But he wanted those confounded gloves and he was afraid to expose himself.

"Haul in the reins," he murmured. "You're old enough to know better. Why bite on old bait? That outfit won't sink in the ground. Meanwhile I can wait just as long as that wall-eyed sucker over there."

Somebody was cached over there. King was pretty sure of it. He drew his gun and waited. The moments dragged, his impatience rose and battled with his wisdom. The fire flared and fell, consumed by the fanning wind. King marked one chunk of wood and set a time limit. When that chunk broke in the center he'd quit fooling and get the gloves. Maybe there wasn't anybody laying back there after all; maybe he was letting the night play on his nerves.

The gun rose and centered. He saw a shadow rear up, directly across the way, waver and march forth. Silas stood in the light, shifting about and keening the air with his nose. Those bright restless eyes seemed to fall everywhere at once and it appeared to King that the man saw him. But Silas shook himself like a dog settling down the fur and shuffled away. Only as he skirted the fire did he catch sight of the gloves lying on the ground. The discovery stopped him instantly. A curious mixture of alarm and astonishment fluttered over his puffy cheeks. Both hands swooped down on the gloves, he looked inside the leather. Then and there the concern died and he laughed silently and walked away.

That single moment of inaction proved his undoing. King Merrick had meanwhile risen and retreated farther in the darkness, traveling the circle until he stood in the man's path. When Silas left the light he ran directly into King's arms. The collision was brief and certain, for Silas offered no resistance at all. At the first touch he crumpled and emitted a weird bleat. King jerked the gloves from the man's grip and shoved him away. Silas hit the ground and rose as if propelled by springs. King waited until the sound of the hanger-on's departure faded into the mists, then went back to his horse and followed the rustlers.

So much was accomplished. The brief

struggle with Silas had taken place in the dark. The man never had caught a sight of King. Silas would report his accident to the Brierlys and they would probably guess King's identity. It didn't matter a great deal, for they already knew that he was on their trail. He might have bound Silas and left him in the ravine for the night, but he thought it not worth the effort. For that matter it might be that the gloves themselves would prove to be useless as clues. Anyhow he had them. They were tucked securely in his coat pocket.

A half hour later King drew near enough to hear the tramping of the rustled stock, and because of the encounter with Silas it seemed to King wiser to leave the direct pursuit and cut into the avenue of Little Finger Draw. They would turn into it later and he could hear them pass by, at the same time doing away with the chance of ambush. This policy he immediately acted on. Up hill and down slope. Into the thick timber and across dew-damp meadows, switching from one to another of the trails that made a checkerboard of the country. King knew almost by instinct when he varied from the proper route, and so he arrived at Little Finger and pushed back in the pines. The cattle were already approaching.

A pair of riders drummed upward and stopped a short way above him. King heard somebody say: "Not tomorrow night. Make it Thursday. Same time, same place."

"Yeah," was the reply.

One of the riders came back and left Little Finger's alley. The cattle were entering the draw at a point higher up. King tarried until the night party were fully embarked on the trail. Once more he followed, mounting higher and higher on this dismal and sinister alley.

But the journey drew swiftly to a close. An hour later the herd debouched from Little Finger into a fast mountain meadow and King knew that the end of the trail had been reached for one night. Satisfied, he turned and struck into the valley. He took the main road and came to Five Echo, which lay asleep in the luminous fog. But the familiar light glimmered through the window of N. Porterfield's restaurant and he went in to help himself to a cup of coffee.

Nancy was still up. Nor was she alone. Dusty Tremaine sat idly at the counter, grinning cheerfully over a piece of pie.

The mark of travel was plain on King Merrick. From boot to hip the brush and the scraping pine bows had drenched him, and here and there the charred logs of the

burn had left a telltale smudge. Nancy Porterfield shook her head with sympathy, but
Dusty's grin widened.

"I don't need more'n eight guesses to figger
where you've been, King," he said.

King waved this aside cheerfully. "I have
been huntin' for the mountain augur bird,
which is a shy creature and seen only at
dark o' night. You'd be astonished to know
how beauteous a creature said bird is." He
looked more closely at Dusty. "Old man
Spring chased you away from his front porch
finally, uh? How come *you* got damp by
ridin' down the trail?"

Dusty winked at Nancy. "I been huntin'
for augur birds too. Took the short cut from
Spring's for a cup of coffee. Better have
one. Ridin' home with me?"

"I guess so."

Nancy poured coffee for both of them.
"You boys ought to get more sleep," said
she, shaking her head.

"You're up pretty late yourself," replied
King.

"Oh, me." Her small square shoulders rose.
"It doesn't matter about me. I don't have
to work all day with the herd."

She was quieter than usual; graver and
indefinably sad. King, bent over his coffee,
felt the long and full scrutiny from her gray

eyes. Dusty Tremaine murmured a joke he had overheard and chuckled to himself, never noticing the change in Nancy Porterfield. King looked up to her and thought he saw a mute appeal. Something had come up that troubled her.

"Let's go," said Dusty, swinging off the stool.

King was building a cigarette. On the moment the stillness of the town was disturbed by a quivering and a drumming. Dusty's head reared and his eyes flashed with the brilliance of an aroused excitement. "Who's comin' in at this time o' night?"

A group of horsemen swirled down the street, a shot went rocketing up as a signal and as King's hand whipped across the lamp top and snuffed out the flame, a series of bullets splintered the front wall of the restaurant, above their heads.

King flung himself over the counter and in front of the girl. "Down to the floor, Nancy!"

The marauding party were carried past by the momentum of their charge. Another bullet cracked at the street's end and marked the outfit's returning.

"Get to the floor!" repeated King. He felt the girl sinking.

Dusty shouted angrily, "What pack of fools — "

King leaped the counter again and wrenched open the door. The party outside had split asunder and were veering here and there, seeming to post a guard about the restaurant. King challenged them. "Who's that? You dam' fools, don't you know there's a woman in this place? You're a pack of yellow cur dogs! Go riddle some other house!"

"Who's talkin' so proud?" came from the street.

Rolf Brierly said that. King would have known the voice anywhere. But before he could speak again Dusty Tremaine crowded the doorway and issued his own challenge. "Tremaine and Merrick. Sounds like Brierlys out there. You boys want to make a fight out of it? By Jodey, we're willin'!"

He ripped the gun from his holster and placed a shot across the street.

"Wait a minute," ordered King. "Let's see what they're after. Don't lose your head."

"They can't run this town," grumbled Dusty. "And they ain't got me buffaloed, either." But he held fire, waiting for an answer that seemed very long in coming. The Brierlys were arguing softly among themselves. Presently Rolf Brierly spoke up.

"It ain't my habit to let a bluff go by.

Don't get no mistaken ideas about it. But we ain't after either o' you dudes — not tonight. We'll settle this argument when we got more time. Smoke that in yore brown papers. Come on, boys."

The riders collected from odd angles and raced away, bound southward to the Five Draws. Lights sprang into windows and townsmen came to the street. Dusty embarked on a long and grumbling tirade. "Why not lay some of that gang in the dust? Now or later. It's shore bound to come."

Nancy Porterfield lit the lamp. King noticed the deep and pinched somberness of her features. Dusty too seemed lacking a little of his usual ruddiness. As for himself, King suppressed the hot, driving anger and nodded. "Let's go home. Nancy, you better turn in. They'll pay a long overdue bill, mark that. And they won't be much longer delayed in doin' it, either. Good night, Nancy."

Dusty went out. The girl raised an arm. "Good night, King. You take care of yourself. It was *you* they were after!"

"I don't get all the uproar," said he. "Something there I don't catch. Well, it'll come out soon enough. Nancy, I hate to poke my nose into places it ain't wanted. But if you ever want to divide that trouble — sure I see it — don't forget me."

She tried to smile. The crooked, wistful tilt of her lips somehow gripped King's heart and woke the anger afresh. "I will, King."

King went out and got in the saddle. Dusty was chuckling again. "For a minute I figgered we'd make medicine. Don't like to see it postponed too long. Just my luck to be way off nowhere when the fightin' starts."

After that they rode in silence. At the ranch they turned in. King thought about the gloves secure in his pocket. The first thing in the morning he'd look them over. So, weary to the bone, he slept until the cook's triangle roused him in the gray twilight. The gloves still occupied his mind. Washing up he slipped to the back of the bunkhouse and took them from his pocket.

They were ordinary gloves — buckskin tips and a tough leather flare into which had been sewed bright beadwork. Three quarters of the punchers wore them when not in the middle of ranch work. King turned back a cuff of the right hand glove and looked inside. A name, deeply etched by a hot nail, riveted his attention. He looked at it for a long moment — a moment in which he forgot to breathe, and in which a chill ran up and down his body. Very quietly he turned the cuff away. That name was Dusty Tremaine.

Chapter Six

To some people a crisis brings numbness and lethargy. In others it evokes a startling, uncanny clarity of mind. During that bleak and tragic moment King Merrick's thoughts flashed across the whole panorama of the preceding thirty-six hours, and before his loyalty woke to make excuses and alibis for Dusty a chain of guilt had been wrought around his handsome, restless partner. It was created out of a dozen circumstances and words and hints that previously had meant nothing at all to King. Dusty's night riding; the suspicion of the ranchers themselves, which they had so carefully hidden from King; their demand that King take oath; Dusty loitering by the saloon and speaking to somebody out in the shadows; Dusty half-heartedly defending the Brierlys at one time, and then again declaring war against them; Dusty's own warning that King had better stay clear of Brierly country; and Dusty, wet with the night fog, idling in Nancy Porterfield's place directly after the rustling. The glove and its identifying name, strung all these facts together to damn the man he so completely loved and trusted.

It was natural that King should instantly react against the evidence. "The Brierlys planted the gloves where I'd find 'em," he told himself. "They put Dusty's name in the cuff to throw suspicion the wrong way. By god, I don't believe it!"

Deep in his heart King did believe it. Looking up to the gray morning sky he bitterly arraigned himself for suspecting his old-time partner. He'd go around, hand the gloves to Dusty. And his partner would explain.

King started around the bunkhouse and stopped, feeling like a man that had been trapped in a death pit. Only then did he remember his oath to the cattlemen. So he turned and tramped backward and forward along the narrow wall, fighting a terrific battle with his impulses. There was no particular phrase in that oath forbidding him to give Dusty the gloves. He would be saying nothing, telling nothing.

This last thought wakened a slow, balked anger. If they had suspected Dusty why had they picked on him, King Merrick, to track down a best friend? It wasn't fair. They had tricked him. They had roped him in by using fine words about his honesty and his ability, and all the while they had known they were putting him up to crucify Tremaine and in turn to be crucified himself.

"All right — I'll play the hand out," King decided. "But when I tell them what I've discovered my job's ended. Then I'll stand by Dusty and see them all in hell!"

The anger simmered and died, leaving him weary and discouraged. He was just talking to make echoes, nothing more. He was a humble man and his guiding light had been an honest one. It was too late now to change, to take the part of a wrecker. The character built up over twenty-odd years was too strong to be broken in a moment's despair. He had to see this thing through, clear down to the final bitter end. Swinging, he lifted his bronzed face to eastward where the mists glistened to the promise of a fresh warm sun. His shoulders rose and dropped and he started around the bunkhouse — to find Dusty Tremaine standing at the corner and watching him in plain puzzlement.

"What's the matter with yuh, King?" Dusty asked. "Been eatin' the wrong brand of oats?" His restless eyes took in the gloves King held so tightly and he grunted. "Say,

I been lookin' all over hell's half acre for them ga'ntlets. Find 'em in your bunk?" He reached forth to take them. King withdrew his arm, eyes drilling into Dusty.

"Not on my bunk, Dusty," King drawled.

Tremaine's memory had played him false for the moment. Now it served with a terrible truthfulness. He remembered. He took a step back and on the instant his whole face was frozen by an ivory pallor that seemed to mirror a complete paralysis of soul and body. His head was tipped at an angle, his teeth flashed with a nervous grimace. He glared at King with so haunted and savage a look that it seemed as though he meant to drive forward and destroy.

King distinctly saw Tremaine's eyes shift color, the transformation was incredibly violent. All the easy going, reckless good humor was consumed on the spot. Dusty's face was to King the face of a total stranger. His nerves warned him to be alert and he steadied himself, not sure but that Tremaine meant to spring upon him.

Another man in King's boots and Tremaine might have done so. But the ancient ties between these two were strong. The next moment Tremaine had turned and vanished around the corner with a sinuous twist of his body. King followed in time to see his

88

one-time partner riding like a wild man across the meadow toward the Spring ranch.

King ate his breakfast silently, feeling the curious glance fastened on him by Pack Mac-Gabriel. Later Pack loitered on the porch, saying nothing yet conveying the impression he expected news. King came to the porch, head tilted over a cigarette. When he raised his face he saw an unusual severity imprinted upon the ranchman's features, a severity that only matched his own expression.

"Well?" grunted Pack.

"I'm ridin' into Five Echo," murmured King, "to sort of work things out in my head. It's all over but the fightin', Pack. All over but that."

"You found the traitor?"

"I found him," answered King, the words brittle and harsh.

"What his name? He's a dead man the minute you identify him."

"I'm ridin' into Five Echo," repeated King, "to clear up my head. Meet me there a little before sunset with a good-sized posse."

"What's the traitor's name?" insisted Mac-Gabriel, growing white about the mouth.

"I'll tell you at Five Echo."

MacGabriel rose. "Merrick, I'll ask you to remember yore solemn oath to us. If that dam' renegade, whoever he is, gets wind of what you know and skips the country before we catch him — "

"I hold myself liable for him," droned King. "If he goes away I'll bring him back. No matter where he goes or how far he goes. As for my oath, I'm rememberin' that, Pack. Meet me at sunset in Five Echo with the posse."

"Yore plumb sure of everything?" demanded MacGabriel. King observed that the ranchman's hands were shaking. He had never seen MacGabriel so aroused. It was death for Dusty Tremaine.

"I'm as sure as I am of bein' alive. But I want a little time to think before I send somebody down to the brimstone pit. Sunset, Pack."

"I will have thirty men there, ready to travel. And I ride myself, if it's the last time I fork a horse this side of Jordan."

King nodded and walked to the corrals. Presently he was pursuing the trail down to the valley highway. It was a clear and beautiful morning; the sun broke through the mists and warmed the world.

Dusty Tremaine never halted his mad gait across the meadows. He rode as if the devil were at his heels and the farther he went the more ruthless he was with the spurs. When Dusty arrived at the Spring place he jumped from the horse and ran to the front door. Lolita had seen him cross the yard and come to the porch, smiling with that frank and gay brilliance so characteristic of her. The smile soon disappeared. A single glance at Dusty foretold trouble. He was dripping with water from his headlong passages of the creek fords. He was still white about the face and the look in his eyes drew a startled cry from the girl.

"Dusty — what's happened?"

"Come out to the corrals, girl. I've got to talk to you." He had never been so rough or so blunt with her. Both hurt and worried she followed.

"Dusty, wait for me! I can't run! What's the matter?"

He appeared not to hear her. Nor did he stop until well beyond the corrals. Then he turned and looked around him with a strangely hunted look.

"I've got to get out of here, Lolita," Dusty almost gasped. "I'm sayin' good-by."

"Out of where, Dusty?"

"Out of the valley!" said he. "No time to lose. By God, Lolita, I hate to go!"

"Why do you have to go, Dusty?" she asked, her voice full of dread. "Have you had a quarrel with somebody? Dusty — have you *killed?*"

"Killed? I wish it wasn't any worse than that," he said. "No. But I nearly pulled a gun on my best friend this mornin'. May the Lord curse me for it. Lolita, I won't ever be seein' you again — think of me a little — don't you judge too hard. I've been rustlin', girl. And I'm caught!"

"Dusty!"

The wild despair quelled his turbulence. He bent forward and took her small shoulders between his big hands. "A man never learns anything till it's too late. You're hurt worst in this jam. Hurt more than me. King's hurt more than me. I've been a dam' fool and it don't do me any good to find it out now."

"Dusty, I don't believe it!"

"Well, it's true," said he, turning morose. The man shifted from one mood to another rapidly, unable to control his temper and take a definite stand. "Started last fall after King pulled out. I've been workin' with the Brierlys, laggin' stock up to the ridge for them to take on. King was sent out by the cattlemen this spring — "

"Oh, Dusty, why did you turn crooked when everything was so bright?" she asked, her voice pleading. "Didn't you think, didn't you *think?*"

He grew angry. "Shore I thought. That's the trouble, I thought too cursed much. I was to marry and support you. How far could I get on a puncher's wages? I'm a proud man, Lolita, and I figured you ought to have the best. I figgered to make an easy stake and start my own outfit. More than one rancher in this valley started that way. But I'm the fellow who gets caught. King was too slick. Now I'm bustin' the breeze before a posse gets me. Lolita — "

While he spoke, Lolita Spring watched his eyes. And in the interval a tremendous change occurred in the relations of these two people. Dusty had always been the masterful and the dominant one. He had swayed her; he had made her cry or laugh at the will of his impulses. Stripped of his old-time manner he made a sorry figure. He had his back to the wall, he was beaten. There was no fight in him. The girl saw this and she knew that, although she would never cease to claim him, he never again could bend her life to suit his own.

"You are not going to run away, Dusty," she said quietly.

"No? I'm to stay here and have my neck stretched, uh?" he sneered. "I'm sorry, girl. It's another bright dream broken."

"It's all very well for you to say that!" said she, growing angry. "But what about me? Dusty, you are a fool! But I still love you, and if you're not going to fight for yourself I am going to do it. I won't see everything broken up. I just won't see it."

"A rustler's got no chance in this country," he muttered.

"You'll have no chance if the valley finds it out," she replied. "But supposing King doesn't tell what he knows?"

Dusty shook his head. "I know King. He'll go through with a bargain if it kills him."

She looked toward the corrals. "Dusty, you ride down to the brakes by the bend of the river. Stay there until I come."

"Where you goin'!" he demanded suspiciously.

"To see King," she replied. "I am going to make him keep this a secret. I am going to tell him that you will never again do a crooked thing, that I am going to marry you and see that you are straight the rest of your life. He will believe me. He's got to believe me."

"He won't," repeated Dusty. "I saw his eyes this mornin'. Lolita, I'd rather take a shot in the heart than see that again. There ain't nothin' I can say or do which would change him. He's a kind man — there ain't a finer one in the valley. But he'll go through with this. I know King. You ought to know him that well too."

"I do," said she, hardly above a whisper. Color came to her face. "But King will do as I ask him. He — he loved me, Dusty."

Tremaine flushed. "Now look here, Lolita, I won't have you tradin' on that. It ain't right — it ain't decent."

"Beggars can't be choosers. You have tried your hand. It's my turn now."

He seemed old, without spirit. And when he looked at the girl he couldn't endure the expression of her face. He closed the space and took her in his arms, almost crying. "I ain't worth the fight, Lolita. You let me go — forget all about me."

She laid her small hand on his shoulder, reassuring him as she would have done to a small boy. "I wish I could let you go, Dusty. There'd be a longer life for both of us. But I can't! Nothing matters, now, Dusty. Nothing but getting you out of trouble. King will listen to me. He's got to listen! You ride over to the river and wait until I come."

Dusty turned away, saying nothing more. Then the girl caught up a horse and saddled. Her father called to her from the house but she galloped across the yard and to the town trail. Presently she took a short cut into the valley road and hurried past the white mail boxes, repeating over and over one phrase. "He's got to listen to me! He's got to!"

She ran through the covered bridge and saw King Merrick riding slowly toward her, his clean and sharply chiseled features raised to the fresh sun.

Chapter Seven

As they came face to face there was a long period of silence. Lolita had never seen so clearly the flint and ice side of King's nature, never before had found so harsh a furrowing of his cheeks.

"Dusty told me everything," she said.

"So's he dragged somebody else into the fine mess he made," was the reply. "Where is he now?"

"At our place," said she.

"Hidin' behind your skirts? Where's the man's pride, what's become of his courage. Lolita, he's my friend, yet. But he's a yellow dog if he doesn't play out his own chips without you helpin'."

"I made him, King," she said quietly. "He was going to run away, but I made him hide out until — "

"Yeah. Tremaine can't run far enough to get clear of me. I want him to know that.

I want you to tell him his only bet is to stay right where I can find him when I want him. There's just one human bein' in this valley that stands between Dusty Tremaine and the rope. I'm the one. And he'll play the game with me or I'll slip the knot under his ear myself. Tell him that."

"King — have you told anybody yet?"

He shook his head. A flash of feeling crossed her face, relief and hope and courage all fused together. She seemed to be fighting for her life; and King suddenly understanding her mission, knew that she was fighting for her life. She still loved Dusty. If he died she had no desire to live. That was the nature of Lolita Spring.

"Then you have got to listen to me, King!" she pleaded. "I am marrying Dusty today. He will never do another dishonest act. I will see that he makes a good citizen. We'll both work to mend the damage he's done. King, I swear that we will return as many cattle as Dusty took. Return them at night so that nobody will ever know. You will be the judge to tell us when we've paid off his debt. There will never be a luxury for either of us nor an idle day for either of us as long as you say we still owe. Never! Dusty is in your hands — I am in your hands. He has been wild, King, but he'll settle down with me and be a good man. I know it. And if he pays off everything and serves his parole to you, isn't that enough? You know it is! You've got to give us the chance!"

"What am I to do, Lolita?" King asked, his voice husky.

"Keep the secret."

"I raised my hand, Lolita," he explained, "and gave my solemn word to the cattlemen of the valley. Your dad was one of them. You want me to break my word."

"Oh, what is that compared to Dusty's life!" she cried out, small fists clenching tight and striking the saddle horn. "What is it compared to making him a decent man — to giving *me* some chance for happiness? You know better, King."

She was fighting desperately hard. Never for an instant did her eyes leave his face. She must have seen the tide running against her, for the fire died out of her and she spoke just above a whisper. "King, look at me."

He lifted his head. "Use fair weapons, Lolita," he said.

"You loved me once, didn't you? Listen to me, King. I'll use whatever weapons a woman has. You don't understand how much it means. Dusty's not vicious, not criminal. He wanted to make money for me — and he took the wrong way. He will never do it again. I promise. And if you will let him repay what he owes, if you will keep his secret — " she paused, turning as pale as death. " — if you will do that you can do as you want with me."

King grew red. "What ever gave you that idea about me, Lolita?" he asked. "I ain't built that way."

She had lost. She knew it. A tremendous sigh escaped her. "All men are alike."

Something died in King Merrick then. He gathered the reins of his horse.

"You're a strong girl, Dusty's a weak man," King said. "And he don't deserve you. Why has he got to hide behind your skirts? I'm promising nothing at all, Lolita. You tell Dusty to stay where he is until I come. Maybe I'll come alone, maybe with a posse. I ain't promising. Dusty broke the rules and he can't cry now! If he gets any mercy it won't be on his account but yours. I've sworn to do a chore. I'll do it. And tell Dusty if he runs there won't be enough miles in the world for him to get away."

She made a sorry little figure in the saddle. Drawing her pony aside she watched him pass. The last thing King heard was: "You can't do it, King. There was too much between you and Dusty. Too much between you and me."

"Some things a man can't do," muttered King. "But some things he's got to do."

A man is able to struggle with his heart and mind only about so long, then there comes a time when all logic collapses and he falls back upon the instincts which are strongest in him. So it was with King Merrick. A mile out of Five Echo he dismissed the whole somber train of reasoning with a fatalistic shrug of his shoulders. He would keep his word. Riding into town he dropped off before Nancy Porterfield's restaurant and walked through the door for a cup of coffee.

Nancy was not there. After a period of waiting King called over the partition, and got no reply. Investigating the kitchen he found the stove cold and the coffee pot empty. Being of a practical mind he started a fire and filled the pot, rolling a cigarette to wait out the interval. By and by it seemed queer to him she was so long absent, for Nancy Porterfield had always been a little proud of her restaurant's reputation. It was early for her to be away visiting. And the cold stove indicated that no breakfast had been served from it, which was even stranger. King left the restaurant and pointed toward the saloon. Midway in the street, Tom Juro, the town marshal, came out of a store to beckon him.

"Nancy Porterfield ain't been in the restaurant this mornin', King," said the marshal. "You a-lookin' for her?"

"Sort of," said King. "Hasn't anybody seen her since daylight?"

"Nobody I can find out," replied the marshal. He dropped a ponderous lid. "She's been a-sparkin' with Rolf Brierly, you know. Mebbe she's gone up there to live."

King looked coldly at the marshal. "Just tell me what all you mean by that, Juro."

The marshal felt King's flaring hostility and he qualified on the spot. He wanted no trouble with this man. "Well," he muttered, "mebbe they run off an' got married. That's what I was aimin' at. They got a right, ain't they?"

"It wasn't in your head," snapped King. "You figgered to mean somethin' else. Juro, you're God's most shining example of a tattler. Keep your limber tongue off the women."

"Brierly was in her place last night, King," Juro went on defensively. "Yuh got to admit that. An' he and his poison crew come a larrupin' through town about midnight and stopped by the restaurant — "

"She was still in the restaurant when they

102

left," interrupted King.

"Jus' a minute," said Juro meekly. "Lemme finish. After you and Tremaine pulled stakes, they came back. We'd sorter went back to sleep in town and they laid a fog o' lead around the street so's nobody wanted to come out. But they stopped at the restaurant again. And I figger they took the girl. A leetle while ago I had my wife go into the gal's bedroom back of the kitchen. Bed hadn't been slept in."

"Great Caesars!" King's outraged feelings spilled over on the marshal's head. "And you stand here like a bump on a log! Why haven't you been stirrin' up a party to look around? Here's a woman maybe kidnapped and you pick your teeth and grin about it!"

Juro shifted from one foot to the other, very much disturbed. Finally he raised his palms. "It's the Brierlys, King. Who'm I to tackle that nest o' catamounts? Don't be harsh about it. Figger for yoreself. Supposin' I get too inquisitive. Next thing I know they're a-spillin' out of that condemned black country and disorganizin' me complete. I'm married. I got children growin' up." Seeing that he made little impression on Merrick's anger he grew desperate. "Now listen — mebbe the girl wanted to go with Rolf Brierly. She's been seein' a lot of him. And they got a disgraced preacher in the crowd which could splice a knot."

In a calmer moment King Merrick might have seen the justice in Juro's argument. Now, far more disturbed about the girl than his relations with her called for, every word the marshal said fed King's wrath. And he was guilty of something he never yet had done. He swore at Juro.

"You dam' ignorant galoot," he shouted. "If anything's happened to her I'll cut your ears off! What right have you got to be wearin' a star anyhow?"

King strode back to the restaurant and ransacked each of the three adjoining rooms. Nancy's hat and coat were missing. Her suitcase was gone. Mustering his courage he opened the drawers of the lone bureau, all her personal effects had been taken out. Just two things remained in her bedroom. One was the gun she always carried. The other — and at the sight of it he felt ashamed at this meddling — was a picture of himself taken at a roundup. Who had snapped the camera on him he didn't know; but there it was, away in a corner of the bureau.

King went hastily through the kitchen, laying the coffee pot off the stove, and ran out of the place to his horse. Riding past Juro he flung out a crisp order.

"I'm goin' into the draws," he said. "If I ain't back by sunset when Pack MacGabriel and his crowd comes through here you tell them where I am. And keep your mouth shut about it to the town. Likewise see you're right on the spot to repeat what I'm sayin' to Pack. Does that sink in, Juro?"

"Yes sirree bob. I'll do jest exactly like you want, King," the marshal replied. "Now don't you harbor no animosity towards a poor cadger like Tom Juro. It ain't fitten a stout young chap like you should measure an old broken down man like me. A pint is a pint and a quart is a quart. Don't you try to fit me into a quart measure, bekase they'll be a lot o' room in the jug when yore done pourin' Tom Juro in. I got a family. I got — "

He was still talking when King Merrick flung his horse through the street and out along the valley road. King rode directly into the timbered reaches lying between the town and the mouth of the draws; and the farther he rode the greater was his impatience and his fear.

Juro's suggestive gossip stung him badly, it outraged his sense of propriety. Whatever the reasons were that prompted Nancy Porterfield to meet Rolf Brierly in the recesses of the Middle Draw, they were honest reasons. She was a girl of mystery; and folks always drew distorted tales from such mystery. It was remotely possible that she had willingly gone with the Brierlys in the middle of the night, but no matter how often King Merrick's questing thoughts returned to this possibility he rejected it. If she had gone that way she had gone at the point of force. He remembered the drawn and anxious look in her eyes the time he had come upon her by the bridge of the Middle Draw. Somehow the Brierlys were unpleasantly connected with her life.

King reached the section of land he had filed on and crossed the small meadow. The sun sparkled on the creek and for a moment warmed his cheeks. Up the trace of the Middle Draw he pressed, crowded to either side by the sullen rock walls and the dense brush. The sun fell behind, unable to penetrate the solid growth of trees. Winter still gripped the draw country, water trickled down the rock faces, and at intervals dark tunnels ran away into the forest. The Brierlys were a dour clan and they inhabited a land exactly suiting their temperament — a cheerless, somber area filled with outlaw pockets and dank, dismal reaches that few men had ever penetrated.

King Merrick was one of the few valley men who had scouted the land of the Brierlys. Therefore he knew what lay ahead of him. Instead of going the full length of the Middle Draw he turned aside some three miles deep in the hills and pursued what appeared to be a blind alley between the pines. The undergrowth clogged the heels of his horse, overhanging bows swept his face.

A quarter hour of this brought King to the river at a place where it flowed lazily. Above was the roar of falls; below a canyon cramped the water and sent it spraying high. He crossed and climbed a precipitous trail. Somewhere in that tangled obscure country he sought and found the trails he needed. About mid-morning King rested his horse on a bluff, concealed in the background of trees, and looked down upon the roof of the Brierly clan's log house.

Valley legend had made of the place a tremendous and almost impregnable fortress. Such is the imagination. In truth it was but a rambling two story affair of stout pine logs, with wide wings and an overhanging balcony all around. Winter came early and lay severely upon these hills; therefore enclosed runways connected the main house with the barn and all out sheds. It faced the river, across which ended the trail raising out of the Middle Draw — at this spot King Merrick eventually would have arrived had he not turned away from that draw earlier. A cable ferry traversed the river. A small clearing lay around the place. To the rear was the bluff upon which King Merrick stood.

King's first business was to look for Nancy Porterfield's horse; and he soon enough found it standing saddled by a corral. The discovery, as much as he expected it, both startled and enraged him. He swept the whole clearing for some point to which he might secretly descend and so command the house at a closer range. A bent and feeble man crawled around from the front and dallied in a patch of sun. At that moment King heard the crackling of a twig behind him and the voice of Silas saying, "It's him."

King flung himself about, reaching for his gun. Silas crouched beside a tree, his bright bird-like eyes dilating. He seemed on the verge of flight, as he always appeared to be. Next to him stood a gaunt and saturnine member of the Brierly clan. He commanded King with a revolver.

"Waited all mornin' by the lower ford," grumbled the Brierly. "Knowed yuh'd cross it. Jump down. Hands elevated celerious.

Higher yit. Silas, ketch his hoss and lead it ahaid. Turn about Mister Merrick. We don't 'low visitors to tote artillery." Still murmuring he closed upon King's back and jerked free the holstered weapon. Silas slid down the bluff face with the horse. The Brierly said "go long brave now," and King marched ahead.

Some kind of signal rocketed across the clearing and rebounded from the bluffs. Immediately the clearing was filled with members of the clan, some coming from the house, others slouching out of the barn. They stood at odd angles as King marched toward them, eyeing him with a gleaming, vindictive triumph. Yet no single word of either anger or malevolence escaped them. They were brutal men and lawless men but the discipline of Rolf Brierly rooted them where they stood. Silas cackled gleefully, whereat one of the clan silenced him with a single harsh phrase. A woman came out of a side door with a pan; she turned her head to look at King and then, her face blanching, she screamed, dropped the pan and threw her apron over her face. The incident impressed King with a terrible vividness and played tricks with his nerves. His guide murmured, "Around the corner, Mr. Merrick and in the front door." King obeyed, crossed the threshold and confronted two people — Rolf Brierly and Nancy Porterfield.

The master of the clan sat at his ease in a chair by the great maw of a fireplace. He grinned at Merrick, a kind of frank and cynical grin; he twisted his slack body in the chair and sent King's captor off with a brief nod.

"Howdy, Merrick. Put yore han's down and rest. Sorter expected one of my houn's would ketch a scent of yuh. Kinda figgered yuh might be on the lady's trail. Heard that woman out there screamin' at yuh? Strangers always affect her thataway. She lived in the valley considerable years back. We took her away from yore country an' brought her here to soften the surroundin's. That's been ten-fifteen years ago, but she ain't ever exactly got over her bashfulness yet. Sit down. Have a smoke. It's a little bit chilly outside."

Chapter Eight

Nancy Porterfield sat on the opposite side of the fireplace, her hands folded in her lap. When King saw her eyes a heavy burden dropped from his mind. All morning he had been fighting an uneasy doubt. Now he knew she had never come to the Brierly house of her own free will. And because of the relief he felt King grinned at Rolf Brierly and drew a chair near the welcome fire. "When you want visitors, Rolf, you sort of go out and take 'em, don't you?"

"I pick and choose," rumbled Brierly, patently enjoying the situation. "Consider yoreself honored, Merrick. It's the first time you ever saw my place. You can count the number of men that have seen it on the fingers of one hand."

King rolled a cigarette. "Slight error in the statement. I've had a look at your roof top before."

Brierly's pleasantry vanished. He sat upright, one big paw smashing the arm of the chair. "Yore lyin' Merrick. Nobody can get through my guards without bein' seen."

"I saw your guards first. One was asleep on the river bank. I slid by the second one."

Rolf Brierly's face turned black and foreboding. "If I knew which men it was that day I'd strip 'em to the waist and lay on the lash. Well, you wasn't so clever this time, my friend."

"That's right," agreed King. "I was in some hurry to get here."

"Why?" demanded Brierly, settling back in the chair.

"You know why, Rolf," King stated. "I just came to tell you it was a piece of business you can't get away with. The valley's let you take your livin' off its herds, but it draws a line on kidnappin'. Your judgment played you wrong this time."

"What's yore valley worryin' about?" jeered the clan leader. "Beef is valuable — it's food and money. But a woman's only a trinket. Anyhow, I didn't take yore woman, did I?"

"You've stepped across the mark," replied King, no longer cheerful. The clan leader's free and easy estimate of Nancy Porterfield stuck in his craw.

"I reckon I got to remind you, Merrick, that it ain't in yore power to do anything about it," Brierly studied King with a long, narrowing glance. "It ain't like yuh to bust so easy into a trap. It don't seem right. Yore a shrewder man than that." His rough voice sailed upward, challenging and peremptory. "What's behind this? What sort of a decoy duck are you anyhow?"

"Let it ride," murmured King.

"Yeah? You ain't puttin' no bug on me. None. I don't get scared easy. If they's a party comin' behind yuh it won't ever reach my front door. Yuh mean to tell me the valley men have got nerve enough to brace me? Why, I'll take my men down there and rip Five Echo apart. I'll burn it to the ground. The valley wants to leave me alone."

"You've stepped across the mark," repeated Merrick with a monotonous insistence.

"I heard that before. But the valley's waited too long. No two men in the valley is equal to one o' my boys. I'm a match for three alone. I've got an imagination, Merrick. I have built me a plan. I make a long shadow on the ground, my friend."

"When a man gets proud of his shadow he's due for a spill," countered Merrick. "When you lay flat, Rolf, you're only six by two. And all graves is six feet beneath the earth."

It irritated Brierly. At the same time it touched the braggart pride in him. He turned his attention toward the silent Nancy and spoke very brusquely. "I'm trainin' a lady to my taste. Watch how a Brierly does it. Stand up, girl!"

The room went black to King Merrick. He was on his feet, stretching his long arm at the clan leader. "You're pilin' up the score, Brierly! You'll answer me for it!"

"Sit down before yuh get a bullet in yore neck," grunted the clan leader. There was a shuffling of boots behind King. He threw a glance over his shoulder to find another of this sullen family standing in the door, revolver pillowed on a raised forearm.

Nancy Porterfield lifted her head bravely and pressed her lips together. She shook her head at King and rose. Into her dark eyes came a scorn and it poured out upon the clan leader. She made a figure of courage standing thus.

Rolf Brierly rubbed his jaw and said, "Sit down. I been teachin' her that trick all mornin', Merrick. Valley women are too proud. Our womenfolk dig and dredge and tend to the animals. This girl, belongin' to any other Brierly would do the same. But she's mine. And I have built me a plan."

He was enjoying himself immensely. For a little while he watched them, letting the silence build up a suspense. The clan leader shifted his body.

"I got an imagination, and it's run me ragged," he said. "So I built me a plan. I aim to spread out. I aim to assume control of the valley from ridge to ridge, clear down to Fire Rock. I aim to make life one long hell for every soul in it. They'll fight — and I'll lick 'em. Then they'll move out. Some of yore fine punchers will crumble and come over to me. I'll use 'em. I could use you, Merrick. Yore as good as a Brierly. You got imagination too and it'd be a comfort to have you around to talk with. I believe I'd split shares even. Now there's an offer."

The man seemed to mean it; he seemed sincere in his declaration. During the recital he had lost the sullen and amused indifference. His whole face lighted with interest; his dark eyes flamed. King said nothing at all. Brierly went on.

"Right here is the center of my empire, by Jobey. Nobody can attack me here and come out with a whole shirt. They'll get discouraged. I'll drum out at night and rustle 'em clean. I've started it already. I'll send lead through their windows, I'll destroy their sleep. And they quit by and by when more funerals have occurred. And then it's my territory. Ridge to ridge, Fire Rock to the top peaks behind me. I'll fill it with cattle. I'll have riders spread around four hundred square miles." He paused a moment to create a fitting frame for the next declaration. "And I'll sit here and let my imagination run around the edges of what I got. It'll have ample room then. It won't be crowded none. The girl will be old Rolf Brierly's woman."

King reached for his cigarette papers and dryly broke into the dream. "You have forgotten that small item known as the law, Brierly."

"The law!" shouted the clan leader scornfully. "What's that? It ain't touched me yet has it? The country's dead scared of me. It's willin' to let me stay inside my premises. I'll just enlarge 'em."

He had finished. He had revealed himself and now more practical things crowded out the vainglory. He rose and kicked open a pair of doors leading off the main room. A table was set for dinner. Rolf Brierly grunted at his henchman by the door. That man ran out. A triangle echoed along the high noon stillness. Rolf Brierly signalled to his forced guests with a kind of travestied courtesy.

They sat down beside him at the head of the table and watched the clan gather in. King thought he would have recognized them all. But it filled him with a complete surprise to find the number of faces he had never seen abroad in the valley. A dozen of the stout and saturnine fellows had ridden into Five Echo from time to time. But there was almost another dozen men, some old, some very young, whose names and countenances were alien to him. These had never ventured out of the black and rugged hills in the last ten years. If they had he would have known them. They were, to put it brutally, prisoners within the walls; their lives beat the small circle. It seemed incredible.

Rolf Brierly laughed, shrewdly divining Merrick's state of mind. "Yuh never figgered I could muster this many, uh? Well, they's a few more out on guard. This place never sleeps. Night or day somebody is watchin'. I told yuh I'd surprise yore valley friends."

After that nobody spoke. They ate in haste and went out. Presently King and the girl were in the living room again, with Rolf Brierly grinning from the doorway. "Enjoy yoreselves. I ain't a jealous man. Go have a look around the premises. But don't step across the boundary lines. Yuh mebbe don't figger anybody's watchin' — but that will be yore mistake. I'm goin' to investigate a little about your comin' this way."

He disappeared and King heard his curt, harsh tones falling around the yard. Horses drummed this way and that. Through the door King saw the clan leader and three others crossing the ferry to the head of the Middle Draw trail. He rolled a smoke in complete silence.

The girl at length broke the silence, lifting her eyes to him. "King — what are you thinking about me?"

He shook his head. "I am thinkin' of how to get you out of here, Nancy."

"You're thinking of something else," said she.

"I threshed that out on the trail. You're honest. That's all I want to know. As for departin' from this — "

He was on the point of telling her that the posse would be coming along after sunset. Then his questing glance saw a door over at the far corner of the room standing ajar and swinging slightly on its hinges. So he avoided that topic, repeating, "I never doubted you had a good reason to talk with the Brierlys."

"You've got a right to know," she answered. "King, I am glad to hear you say you don't doubt me. You don't know how much that means! I didn't come here of my own accord. They came back last night after you were gone and took me. But I had seen Rolf Brierly three or four times previously. I had asked him to meet me in the woods. There was something he could tell me. He promised to tell me — and never did. You don't know how hard it was to face him alone!"

"I can make a broad guess at it," muttered King.

"I wanted to tell you that day," she went on, "but my pride wouldn't let me. I have been fighting alone for so long that it's come to be a sort of religion. And I have never been able to trust anybody. King, my right name is Nancy Ware. Up until three years ago I lived in Augusta, Maine. My mother died at that time and I came west to find out something that's been a family tragedy to us for fifteen years. I came west to find what has become of my father, Edwin Angus Ware. He left Augusta when I was four years old. Maine is a rocky land for a small farmer and dad, according to my mother, was restless and improvident. So he left, telling her he would find something better in a newer country. Fifteen years ago. Mother kept the farm and waited. He wrote three letters, each one half a year apart. Then — " Her voice trailed off to silence. Her clear, white face tipped forward, mirroring something of the tragedy of that long gone history. "Then the letters stopped and we never heard from him again."

King repeated the name to himself. "Edwin Angus Ware. Nobody lived in the valley by that name durin' the last ten seasons."

She broke through his talk, as if she never had heard him. "King, you don't know the things women can think about in a case like that. When I grew old enough to see for myself I recall that I never saw my mother smile. She told me. And we used to wonder. Was he alive and crippled and helpless? Or had he died and been buried in some forgotten grave? You don't know how the uncertainty hurt us, year after year. Always the same questions and the same doubt. Or had he just gone away and left us to ourselves? It hung over us every day. And when mother died I said I would come out here and hunt until I found out what had happened. No matter how long it took. So I came."

King shook his head. "Seems to me that for one girl you've had more'n your share of trouble."

"Sometimes," said she, "it has been hard

to smile. I went to each of the three places from which his letters had been sent. One in Kansas, a second in Oklahoma, the third from a town a hundred miles south of here — Burnt River. And finally, after six months I found a man, an old man, on a ranch outside of that place who had known my father. He hadn't seen dad for more than ten years. But he told me that dad had a partner and that the two of them punched together and finally had ridden north together. He said that if I could find this man he would know all about dad. The name of the partner was Dolf Brierly."

King raised his head sharply. "Yeah? Dolf was the first of that clan to come here and settle Five Draws. He died four years back. Rolf's his son."

"I found that out after I had traced the Brierly name. It wasn't very hard — that part of it. The Brierlys are known. So I came here and started this restaurant. I couldn't ride into these hills and meet Rolf directly, so I thought I'd see him sooner or later in the restaurant. You understand, the nearer I got to the source the more cautious I became, the more secretive. I had discovered that direct questions aren't popular. I had to go at it roundabout. And I couldn't broadcast my mission. For if dad were still living and heard I looked for him — what was he apt to do? After so many years he might slip away and the long hunt would be wasted. So I finally met Rolf. And I asked him. He promised to tell me, but he kept putting it off, making me meet him time after time. And here I am."

"He ain't said anything yet?"

She shook her head. "But he knows something! I feel that in my heart. He knows — if he would only tell!"

"We'll chalk that up on the scoreboard, too," muttered King. He rose, unable to be confined longer. "Care to take a walk around the premises?"

She smiled faintly. "Don't take my troubles to heart, King. I know the kind of a man you are. You mustn't worry about me like you worried about Tom Juro's wife that time. No, I don't want to face the Brierlys."

King went outside and stood a moment on the porch watching the ferry drawn against the gravel of the far bank. It was of the common type. A cable stretched from shore to shore and to this cable the ferry was attached by a traveling pulley which in turn was held to the ferry by means of a short guy cable running into a windlass. A turning of the windlass threw either nose of the ferry up or down stream. Leaving either shore the nose pointing out was skewed up slantwise against the current. The force of the water struck the downstream end of the vehicle and shoved it across. At this point the river was shallow and swift and not much more than fifty yards wide. A bridge would have saved time and labor; but it would not have given the Brierlys the security they needed. So the ferry was used. A man stood by the windlass, waiting the return of the scouting party, a mark of Rolf Brierly's discipline and forethought.

King wandered leisurely around the house, measuring all things with a practised eye. None of the clan was to be seen, but a dozen good horses stood saddled by the corral. There was no sign of cattle in the clearing; doubtless these were held in other remote meadows. King continued his circuit, and on the blind side of the house he found Silas.

Silas crouched in a patch of sun, running his hands along the ground like some young boy building an imaginary railroad. He heard King approaching but he failed to lift his head. He seemed gripped by trouble, his body swayed and he muttered unintelligible words end on end. King paused.

"You're among friends, Silas," King said. "Why play dumb when you don't have to do it? Seems to me it'd get tiresome."

Silas shook his head, twining a whispered warning through the grumbling gibberish he spoke to himself. "Go way. They're a-watchin' us. Go way."

King walked off, grinning. "All right, Silas. Play that game if it suits you. Maybe it takes a lot of training to appear simple." There was a pile of wood near the front of the place and King took a seat, watching the river flow past, puzzling out his own part in the coming burst of trouble.

The posse would be along after dark. If they came across the lower ford and dropped off the bluff they'd be running into grief before they got within shooting distance of the house. Rolf Brierly had that alley well guarded. If the men of the posse came by way of the Middle Draw they would be blocked by the river. And then what? In such an event he and Nancy Porterfield were poorly placed.

"I'd like to get her out of that house when dark comes," King reflected. "Anything's apt to happen, none of it good for her. Somehow I've got to get her away. The boys will wreck this joint sooner or later, but it may take time."

King smoked on while the sun went westering. Now and again he idly surveyed the fringes of the clearing and with equal casualness let his attention roam along the log walls of the Brierly stronghold. Silas went away, leaving the yard quite alone to him; but though King could find nobody around the premises he felt eyes constantly watching him. Presently he tired of all this and went back inside.

The girl had gone, probably to some room. King kicked a log into the fireplace and relaxed. Sunset came after an interminable afternoon.

Rolf Brierly returned and the triangle sounded. The clan leader was spilling over with a restless good humor. He bawled up the stairway. "Come on down, woman! We eat on time in this house. You got to learn there ain't any dallyin'. I'm boss — you bet I am. King, my friend, the valley men are made of yella butter. They don't stir. And they won't. Yore in trouble, and nobody to help yuh."

Nancy came down from an upstairs room. Once again the two of them endured a grim somber meal, and once again they dallied by the fireplace. But with the coming of dark Rolf Brierly showed still another side of his nature. He became foreboding and sullen, sending Nancy Porterfield back to her room with a single, angry phrase. "Get out of sight!"

"You'll burn for that, Brierly," muttered King, as cold as ice.

"Who said so?" snapped the clan leader. "Sing humble, friend. I offered yuh a chance to come over with me. Yuh refused it. Now yuh take what scraps I'm pleased to give. Yore life here depends on the twiddle of my fingers. Yore a problem — and I don't like problems. The boys want to shoot yuh down and I ain't that far advanced in ideas yet. They ain't no place in my plan for a man with as much nerve as you got. It balls things up. I ain't decided what to do about it, so the less you say the better off yore goin' to be. Now hustle up them stairs and take the room to the left of the landin'. I'm cookin' up some poison bait for yore friends." He grinned maliciously at King's interest. "Shore I know they're a-comin'. What do you reckon I spent the afternoon doin'? I'm layin' a trap on the butte. Go upstairs."

King went up and entered the room assigned to him. A lamp glimmered on the table, a newspaper, long past issued, was spread as if to invite him. These things he took in with a passing glance and went to the window. Below the window stretched the roof of the side porch. It was but a step

126

down and a small jump thence to the ground; beyond was utter blackness. And in that blackness King well knew that a guard watched him. So he turned back, swinging on his heels as if to find encouragement in the blank walls.

King heard men riding out from the house, around on the far side. It sounded as if they went toward the rear bluff. He heard something else, nearer at hand. Turning, he found the white and puffy face of Silas pressed against the window. The man's arm made an upward gesture and King, strongly warned to be on his guard, went over and lifted the sash. Silas pulled himself through hurriedly and lowered the sash, the next moment shrinking away to a sheltered part of the room. His eyes, always bright, burned with an added brilliance and his face was queerly, weirdly set. One fist swept into his coat and came out with a forty-five. He passed it to King, whispering an explanation.

"Man at the foot of the stairs, watching," Silas said. "Man outside watching. The man outside went into the kitchen a second to get a cup of coffee. I waited for that. Mister Merrick, I'm as sound an' sane as you are. For the Love o' Gawd hurry while yuh got time. Go out the window and crawl to the girl's window. Get her. Drop down and take her away from this stinkin' pit! Hurry, yuh only got a bare minute while Teepee's inside the kitchen with his coffee!"

"Silas, I know you," muttered King. "You're as tricky as a snake. They put you up to this. Some of the boys want to knock me off when Rolf ain't lookin'. I'm obliged, but you go back and tell 'em no."

"No — no!" groaned Silas. Every feature of his face and every muscle of his body seemed to knot up. King had never before seen so terrible and gripping earnestness. "It ain't so! They'll kill me if they find out! I got some pride — I can't stand to see the girl done up! Man, don't look at me while time goes by. He's drinkin' his coffee — he'll be through in a minute! Go on an' get her away from this hell!"

King dropped the gun in his holster. His reason told him to be on his guard, yet the possession of the gun released the reckless energy he had suppressed all the day. And Silas was pushing him toward the window with something like frenzy.

"Silas, if this is a trick — " King began.

"No — no — no! Go on! Time's goin'! Take her south. Circle the bluffs and hit for the canyon of the Appanachee! They's one — "

Silas was interrupted. A shot cracked across

the river, followed by a full volley. King heard a bullet striking the logs outside; and he heard as well the remainder of the Brierlys racing around from all angles of the yard. Over there at the head of the Middle Draw trail waited the posse.

Silas sighed like a weary man. King ran his hand across the lamp globe and snuffed out the light. The time had come; that tiresome afternoon he had nursed a number of plans and now the time was ripe to try one of them. He raised the window, dropped to the roof and, after one moment's intent listening, let himself fall to the ground. The shots had drawn all the guards away from the side. He was secure for the moment; but only for a moment. He could plainly distinguish the main part of the clan come scrambling down the bluff trail. The fight was on and success hung on the one desperate move he aimed to try.

Chapter Nine

There was the fragment of a moon in the sky, but the dim light of it lay behind the high shield of bluff and pine. So this area swirled with vague and palpitating shadows. Crouched by a front corner of the house King Merrick marked all the varying sounds around the place and balanced his own chances by them. Why had Pack MacGabriel advanced along the trail of the Middle Draw and announced himself boldly from across the river? Was this a diversion, meant to conceal a part of the posse's approach by the lower ford and along the rear alley of this grim stronghold? Perhaps. It occurred to King, however, that scarcely any of the men in the posse knew this country. It appeared as if MacGabriel had elected the main trail with the full intent of breaking through the obvious handicaps by plain force rather than to take the chance of being lost or ambushed by a less familiar route.

The full weight of the Brierly clan swept back from the bluff, answering the challenge of the posse. Three or four of those left to guard the house moved near the river. King saw one gaunt form dimly silhouetted against the river's dull silver surface. The others he heard murmuring. Below them the ferry lay, its shore end gently scraping the gravel beach, an indistinct skeleton in the night.

King slid away from the corner of the house and detoured by the Brierlys, slipping softly toward the ferry. At that interval he held his gun high; but as he touched the ferry's end, he jammed the gun in his belt, bent his whole weight against a side post and urged the ferry from its uncertain mooring on the bank. The next moment he abandoned all caution and sprang at the windlass, flipping the guard ratchet free from the windlass and throwing the crank around and around. The clatter beat back along the shore, the ferry swung and trembled against the current. Warning broke the shadows, high and angry. A shot ripped the planking at his very feet, another sheered the water at one side.

"Who's that?" called a voice.

"Merrick, yuh fool!" somebody answered. "Teepee, where you been to let him git free?

131

You'll ketch merry — "

"Get that ferry — !"

The current bore the ferry outward slowly. One of the Brierlys flung himself into the water. King, running to the shore end, felt the man's weight springing against the craft. The shadow of this Brierly reared out of the stream, head and shoulders and torso. For an instant he hung balanced and at that point King drove forward, struck the man fairly and hard, sending him backward and full length to the river's surface. The splash was a signal for the clan, arriving at the beach, to open a wicked, sledging fire. King rolled over to the outer edge of the planking and held himself flat. There were no more attempts made to overtake the craft. The current picked it up and shoved it rapidly into the deep midstream. King swung about and crawled to the other end, calling to the posse on the far bank.

"Pack — hey Pack."

"Merrick?" called the answer.

"Yeah. Leave somebody with the horses," King directed. "Don't waste no time about pilin' aboard this sea-goin' monster. They're apt to try to cut the cable and leave us float into the lower rapids."

No more shots came from the clan. Something happened swiftly and surely over there

— Rolf was stripping himself for that fight he had long boasted he would win. The ferry touched gravel again and the men of the posse waded out to meet it. King jumped to the windlass and skewed the downstream end upward. Pack was beside him, grumbling.

"Got yore word through Juro," Pack explained. "We didn't lose no time. I figgered the worst and I'm pleased to say it's a relief to know yore still sound an' sane. Dam' country. Nobody knew it from Adam's off ox. Figgered we'd have to wade across. How many in that gang anyway?"

"About two dozen good guns," said King. The ferry swayed to the crowding men. "For the love of Saint Peter, how many boys did you bring, Pack?"

"I got thirty-four," announced MacGabriel with grim satisfaction. "And we exterminates that crowd. Root and branch. Then we'll proceed to burn out the nest, down to the last corral pole. I don't want nothin' left. We get that outfit now or we never get it. The valley's got to live in peace and security, somethin' which it ain't been able entirely to do yet."

"It won't be as easy as just sayin' it," muttered King. The ferry swayed to its load. Midstream, King issued a warning. "You boys get down out of the atmosphere. The whole

133

crew over yonder is primed and waitin'. About half of you step to the back side of this hack so the nose of it will go high and dry. When you start off, start sudden and spread out. They'll give way to the house. Somebody give me a handful of shells."

Pack obliged him with the shells. King stepped to the front end and waited. The outline of the Brierly log house appeared out of the shadows. "Be careful, boys. There's a woman upstairs and more women in the back part." The ferry, striking shallow water, made a sheering sound and slackened speed. Still there was no signal of resistance. Silence hung like a dismal and sinister wreath upon the clan area. Gravel scraped, the ferry piled up on the shore.

"Now!" yelled King and threw himself high and dry. The men of the posse crowded after him and shouldered him aside. A fierce and fiery cry of battle went shrilling inward to the house. And from every angle of the yard guns woke and battered against the posse. Powder smoke rolled along the earth; blue flame points danced in the air, unfolding and vanishing, and reappearing again somewhere else.

One stalwart man of the posse died there on the rim of the water, died soundlessly beside King Merrick. The Brierlys, standing on raised ground, had sent their shots a little high and the attacking valley partisans had ducked low in that first impetuous rush off the ferry. But this fellow had scorned to crouch. He had flung himself full-chested into the flailing arc of lead. Then and there King Merrick dropped his scruples. The mildness and the patience that always abided with him, was lost before a raging anger. Never afterwards was he able to remember what he had done in those first moments of fury. He was a part of the crowding valley men, beating inward to the house, always beating inward and knocking apart every attempt of the Brierlys to gather and make a stand at any definite point of the yard. He remembered halting by a corner of the house and reloading. Then he pressed on, fighting like a machine. The wires were down between head and heart in that brief space of time, King obeyed only the instinct to crush and destroy.

When his mind cleared and reason returned he found himself in the center of a mad fight by a long corded pile of wood. It seemed strange to him that he had drifted this far away from the ferry landing. The main contest appeared to be in progress over on the other side of the house, around the barn.

But here he stood with a half dozen or more of his own party, separated from an unknown number of the clan by the wood.

The revolver play at this point subsided. The shadows cloaked surreptitious movement. Those very shadows shifted and seemed to pile up where the threat of trouble was heaviest. King heard a Brierly's stout breathing wheeze through an aperture of the wood.

That was the end of the lull. Those isolated members of the tribe elected to fight again. They swarmed over the top of the wood and down upon the backs of the valley partisans. A muzzle belched in Merrick's face. He was struck by whipping legs and flailing arms. He went down, his face gouging into the damp earth. The man above him took a fleeting grip on his fingers and he felt a bone snap from sudden pressure. He fought free, never daring to fire against the bulk of his own partners. So he closed again recklessly and gripped the unknown Brierly shoulder to shoulder. The man's right arm eluded him. A gun in the fist of that arm threatened his backbone. King tried to shake off the menace of that weapon and succeeded only in drawing it tighter to him.

The danger wrought a vast explosion inside him. He came to his knees, carrying the Brierly likewise up. King pulled himself to his feet with the man locked about him like a crab. He whirled and jammed the fellow full against the pile of cordwood; he heard the unknown one's head snap against the wood. After that he was free and the man lay against the pile, bereft of his weapon. King dropped a knee in the fellow's stomach and challenged.

"What son of an orry-eyed catamount are you, anyhow?" he asked.

He had to wait until the man collected a little air. The reply was half angry, half forlorn. "Teepee Brierly, yuh daggone Greek wrassler! Hoist offen my bread basket. I'm like to partin' in the middle."

"Well, my boy, what you did to me is ample," said King. "You busted a finger, tore enough skin off my face to make a pair of boots, and made some sort of a dent in my spine. I'd sure like to know the brand of milk you was raised on. Never mind your stomach. You won't be eatin' much but bread and water for a spell."

The fight hereabouts had come to an ending. A Brierly beyond the pile was lifting his black and profane curses to the sky. And somebody was hit badly. The outcome of this conflict King couldn't tell.

Teepee Brierly spoke again, with less of

anger than before, and a great deal more sorrow. "Merrick? Why in hell have *you* got to pick on me? Lick somebody yore size for a change. I'm shore a sunk skiff now. Rolf will mash me plenty fer lettin' you slip clear."

"No he won't," contradicted King. "He won't mash anybody."

King heard old man Spring talking down the line. He rose and collared Teepee Brierly. Over by the main house was a sudden flurry. The posse appeared to be making a breech of the place. "Say, Spring, you hold this singed wildcat."

"Yuh." Spring came near and dropped a great paw on the Brierly. "You go ahead, King. I got a bellyful of this affair. I ain't needed yonder anyhow. Me and the boys here will clean up this situation. Somebody's bad hurt. Hey, line up what we got. I want to know — "

Merrick ran across the yard. The front door of the house stood open. Before King reached it a sudden tide of men poured out of it. All other openings in the house seemed to give way at the same moment. King paid no attention to this. He wanted to find Nancy Porterfield and reassure himself. So he went into the main room. A bracket lamp flared high against the wall, fire glowed on the hearth. Over in a corner he heard a man groan and thresh. He started to turn and checked the move. A woman screamed upstairs, a door was thrown wide open.

The lamp's outer edge of light barely touched that upper landing, but King saw distinctly enough the huge frame of Rolf Brierly slide through, hauling a woman after him. It was Nancy Porterfield. Her face formed a dead white oval in the dim light, she was crying in pain and yet trying to suppress the cry. Rolf pulled her to the landing, his grim face bent near her own.

"You wanted to know about yore dad?" he bellowed. "I was a fool for ever botherin' with yuh. Yore too frail and white for a man like me. Yore nothin' but trouble. Wasn't for you Merrick wouldn't never have got this far. I'm tellin' you where yore dad is. He was a yella cur and he's been feedin' on Brierly scraps ever since we broke him. You want to see yore dad? Well, go downstairs and look in the corner. His name is Silas, and he's dyin' from my bullet!"

Rolf straightened his arm. The pressure of it shot the girl across the landing and she fell in a corner out of King's sight. Brierly turned about and for the first time saw Merrick standing silent at the foot of the stairs.

Poised up there, high above King Merrick, he made a formidable and sinister figure. The

139

light of battle smouldered in his black eyes — King saw the flash and flare of them even across the distance, even in the partial shadows obscuring the man. The overflow of that wrath was on Brierly's dark cheeks, the muscles of which ridged out against the stubbed flesh. All the lawless, harsh domineering qualities that had made him supreme in his own clan lay plainly to view. Yet at that moment and with his last brutal blow against the girl to condemn him forever, there was still something in his magnificent disregard for danger that evoked a trace of admiration in the waiting Merrick. The clan leader's fine plan was crumbling. Amid the wreckage he planted his feet and reared his head.

"Well, Merrick." His voice came clear.

"I'm raisin' my gun in a minute," said King. "I will give you time to get your own piece out of the holster."

Brierly's chin sank. He seemed to be brooding over the past. "You and me could've done a lot to this country, Merrick," he said. "Imagination's the thing. You got it. So've I. It makes a man restless, it never lets him alone. All the rest" — his left arm indicated the outer world — "are plain dumb brutes. Do yuh think yore a faster man than me?"

"We'll know in a minute," said King, never stirring.

"It'll be interestin'," mused Brierly. "I'd like to've had you for a pardner."

"Not in a thousand years, Rolf. Not in ten thousand years. You stepped over the line a minute back."

Brierly shrugged his gaunt shoulders. "A woman's only a trinket, Merrick. I can understand fightin' over land or cattle or a yella dog. But God sure must've made us crazy to fight over a woman. As for this — "

"Let that ride," said Merrick, white about the mouth. Brierly's red eyes stared downward. He shook his head.

"Who said you was an easy goin' man?" Brierly wanted to know. "The valley don't know yuh none. I got an imagination and I can see. Yore a killer."

"Yeah — tonight," King snapped, impatiently.

The gunshots swelled outside, a man cried, and silence came pounding down upon the clearing. "They'll be comin' here pritty quick," Brierly went on casually. "My boys didn't fight hard enough. Ever think of death, Merrick? If I had my own choice I don't reckon I'd order an imagination. Well — "

"I'm waitin' for your draw," droned Merrick.

Some of the posse approached the door,

talking. Somebody stood on the threshold, and spoke a single warning. Thereupon the talk ceased and the room was as quiet as a hermit's cell. Brierly appeared cut from stone. His head had dropped and thus shadowed Merrick saw nothing of what passed across the man's face in that long, long moment of suspense.

As for himself, King was cold and nerveless and he saw a woman's face rising in front of him — the grave and clear face of Nancy Porterfield as she had looked up to him one night in the restaurant.

Death hovered on the stairway. Rolf Brierly swayed, nothing more — arm and body and head rising together. The room shivered, the walls beat back the echoes of two shots and above that moment's fury came a piercing cry. Not from Brierly, but from Silas who lay dying beyond the fireplace. Brierly poised on the landing, both long arms sagging. His gun dropped and turned over on the stairs. The man tried to lift his head. It rose half to the dim light and a last sullen, reckless flare sprang out of his eyes. And then he pitched forward, crashing down, falling unchecked the length of that incline and sprawling at Merrick's feet.

At once the place was boiling over with talk and excitement. Members of the posse came streaming in. Nancy Porterfield rose from the remote corner of the landing and ran down, crying: "Dad!"

Merrick put out an arm. She brushed it away and went by him, kneeling by Silas.

"I heard you tellin' Mister Merrick you was lookin' for yore dad," Silas said. "And you told yore real name. Don't think too harsh on yore old man, daughter. I was beat out and I never had courage to come back home. If I see yore mama I will explain — " The rest of his speech went down the endless trail with him.

Merrick turned his back to the girl. Mac-Gabriel stood over the dead Brierly. "He's dead, that's shore certain. Merrick, you did a chore. One more little chore and the housecleanin' is done."

Merrick raised the fist in which he held his own gun. And with his free arm he pulled the weapon clear. Pack stared wonderstruck. "What's the matter with yore trigger finger?"

"One of the Brierlys busted it."

"And yuh braced this gent in that condition? I will be everlastingly — "

"It had to work for me once," said King and swung back to the girl. She wasn't crying but when he found how tight an expression held her face he wished that she could cry.

"This is no place for you," he murmured. Taking her arm he led her into the adjoining room and closed the door. She sank into a chair, Merrick roving around a table and trying to muster up words that would comfort her. Yet all he could think of was that this ending was the easiest. And so, believing in the power of bluntness to cut away trouble, he said as much.

"It's best, Nancy. You can't maybe see it now. But it's best."

"Oh, King, it isn't that so much! He's suffered for his own faults. And now he's out of it. But I'm thinking of all the years my mother waited and hoped and of all the nights that she lay awake!"

"How about yourself?" he demanded gruffly.

"It doesn't matter! I am strong enough to get over it. I have never asked for sympathy."

"There's plenty willing to give you sympathy," he muttered.

"Then — King — I'll ask just a little from you. King, take my hand and hold it. It has been so long since anybody ever has wanted to help me!"

His hard fist closed over her small fingers. "That goes for now or for the rest of my life, Nancy."

She raised her eyes to him and started to speak. But Pack MacGabriel was calling

144

King's name from the main room. He left her and went back to the posse. The room was filled with men. Against the wall all that was left of the Brierly clan stood captured and sullen.

"We're burnin' this shebang to its sills," said MacGabriel.

"Wait a minute," interrupted King. "How about the womenfolks on the place? You can't turn 'em into the woods."

"I found 'em in the kitchen," said Mac-Gabriel. "Only three. And they shore look as if life hadn't nowise agreed. I'd like to take this pack of Brierlys and whip 'em with wet rawhide till they stunk! The women don't want to stick. They want to go outside and get away. Seems like they got relatives somewhere. That leaves this place deserted and I don't propose to leave it open to another bunch of rustlers and renegades. She burns."

King shook his head. "It's too much work to destroy, Pack. I been thinking. My section lays below this. Somebody's got to use this hill country sooner or later. I'm proposin' to take over the house and clearing. It's a good place to establish home quarters."

"Yuh already filed on gov'ment land," objected MacGabriel. "Yuh can't file on any more. This is gov'ment land which the

Brierlys have just took without right. Been squattin' free and easy. Somebody could come here after you got fixed and take it from anunder you."

"I can have somebody else file it for me," decided King. "I got that figured. No burnin'. I'm not stealin' anything. The Brierlys won't be comin' back."

"Not for about twenty years," grunted MacGabriel. "Well, that's all right with me. We'd all ought to be glad to see an honest man nestin' up here. But I shore had my heart set on a bonfire. Now let's get this finished — "

"How do we stand?" somebody asked.

The fire was dying out of Pack. He looked tired. "I reckon we've lost two fine boys. God's will. I dunno just yet how many Brierlys we knocked over. Dunno if any got away. Maybe one or two did. But they ain't stoppin' short of the State line, lay a rope on that." He turned to the other members of the posse. "Let's hustle this thing through. Scout around. Get a couple wagons out of the shed and hitch 'em up. Tie these rustlers. They're goin' straight to the pen. Now about — "

King knew what was coming and he forestalled it by moving away. "I got to see about something," he murmured. On the threshold he turned to catch old man Spring's attention and ducked his head slightly. Spring followed him to the porch.

"I'm not goin' to beat around the bush," said King. "You're willing to go some distance to see Lolita happy, ain't you?"

"I reckon," agreed Spring.

"Would you give fifty head of cattle to see her satisfied?"

"Now listen, you highbinder," broke in Spring, "what's the idea? You demandin' that many cows to marry my girl? Have I got to stock yore ranch for a weddin' present?"

"It ain't me," said King. "Ain't you found out yet she and I ain't engaged?"

That surprised Spring. "Hell, no. Why daggone it, that's a shame! But yuh wouldn't expect her to tell me, would yuh? When I want to find out anything about Lolita I go ask the neighbors. They know plumb sooner than I do. That's raisin' a daughter for you. Who's ranch have I got to stock?"

"You're promisin' fifty head to make her satisfied, Spring? I want that promise before I say a word. I'm just a-tellin' you it means a lot to her."

"I'd sell the ranch if it meant that much to her, Merrick," said the old man, resoundingly, "She's the only daughter I got."

"You got any idea who this inside rustler is?" King asked.

"The valley feller? No. MacGabriel's got a hunch. Nobody else. You know now?"

"Yeah." The answer was so brittle that Spring moved around to get a better look at King's features. "Listen. Your girl is set on havin' Dusty Tremaine. Dusty's my best friend. And I give my word to tell you fellows what I found out. Well, Dusty's the man who did the scoutin' for the Brierlys."

"By God, I'll put a bullet through him! I never had no idea! A-comin' around my girl like a snake in the grass — "

King interrupted. "Ease down. She knows all about it. Dusty told her. He wanted to run off. But she made him stick. She wanted me to keep it a secret. I can't do it. You boys roped me tight and I've got to go through. But I aim to see he pays back what he's rustled for the Brierlys this winter and I aim to ask for a favor from you seven gentlemen. Aim to ask that you all give Dusty another chance. I'll watch him. I'll be responsible."

"Marry Lolita after turnin' crooked?" exclaimed Spring. "What you take me for, Merrick?"

"Either you do that or she'll run off an' marry him anyhow," King explained. "Or if you put a rope around his neck you're going to have a daughter with a broken heart the rest of your life. It means fifty cattle out of your herd if everybody else agrees. That's to pay back."

Spring was struggling with a problem he couldn't master. "King," he asked sadly, "what can a woman be thinkin' about to marry a crook? I don't nowise understand it."

"Nobody else understands a woman either," said King. "You ain't alone. But Dusty ain't a plain crook. He just wanted to make quick money for Lolita. I'm askin' you this — how many old-timers can you name who did a little quick collectin' when they was young? You know plenty of 'em. And those that didn't get caught and quit when they was still reasonable are among our solid citizens right now."

"I don't nowise understand it," repeated Spring.

"She wants him, that's enough. You better make the best of it. She'll make him into a better man. Will you go through with it?"

"I guess I better," said Spring very slowly. "I guess I better. Say, I'd give all I own if it was you, King."

"It ain't to be. That's ended. I'm callin' the other ranchers out here. You talk to them. They'll listen to you better than to me. And you better make it strong. They want Dusty's neck."

"Oh they do, uh?" grunted Spring. That one phrase shifted his whole point of view. There was nothing complicated about his reasoning processes. He would have helped hang Tremaine quite cheerfully up until now. But the fact that his own daughter wanted the man changed his thoughts to a different track. Lolita wanted Dusty; therefore Dusty was the same as her property. And his neighbors wanted to destroy something that belonged to his daughter. He grew belligerent at the thought. "You bring them fellows out here. I'll do the palaverin'. If fifty head ain't enough I'll raise the ante."

"Tremaine will thank you for it," said King, moving into the room.

"To hell with Tremaine. It's my daughter I'm thinkin' about. She's always got what she wanted. That goes now. You bring the bunch out here. But keep it from them punchers. I don't want this to get no farther'n my best friends."

King went from one ranch owner to another and sent them out to the porch. Then, moved by an inner excitement alien to him, he went through to where Nancy Porterfield still sat.

King had meant to say something to her,

something about starting back the trail to Five Echo. That died in his throat. She looked up, her clear face making an oval in the yellow light. It seemed to King that she had been waiting for him to come back. Her eyes met his glance as if she wanted him to read her heart, as if she were opening it to him. He was a blunt man, but that message was too plain to be missed. He put out his hand and she took it, rising from the chair. And he knew then that nothing he could say would express the feeling crowding up — that words would do nothing for him. He could never explain, never hope to translate the crosscurrents in his heart. Therefore he drew her forward and kissed her; the gods were kind when they gave him that inspiration.

Presently he heard her saying, "I didn't lie that time when I said I might be waiting for a man like you. I meant you."

He smiled, a sweet self-deprecatory smile. She drew back to observe it. "King, that changes you so completely. It shows you to me. I know what you are. When I saw you smile the first time, a long, long while ago in the restaurant, I loved you. And I thought it would never do me any good."

"That chapter," said he, solemnly, "is closed. I'm promisin' you it's finished. It's gone and won't come back."

"What do I care?" she said gayly. "You don't have to give any promises. I can see all I want to see in your eyes right now. Look at me! I never gave any man a serious thought until you walked into my restaurant. And then I threw myself deliberately at you."

"I guess the angels sure must be taking care of old King Merrick," he replied, and smiled again. "I am ridin' out to the county seat for a license. I'm comin' right back. We'll be married as soon as the law allows. You bet. And we're movin' up here. I've figured to make a home ranch of this place." Then a more serious thought came to him. "Maybe I'm goin' ahead too fast. Maybe you won't want to live in a place like this, with all that's happened here."

"I want to. It is a start isn't it? It's home. You can't ever understand what a home means to me."

"I can sure make a guess. It sounds sort of good to me. Nancy, I'm a fool for luck."

Pack MacGabriel was calling for him again. King walked over to the door, still holding her arm. He threw the door open and confronted the boss of the Music Box and the ranchers. Pack studied him with an unwonted severity.

"You win, King. No other man in this state could have convinced us. But you win."

"I'm thankin' you."

"Yeah," grunted MacGabriel. He looked from Nancy to King and back again. "Say, King, what I want to know is this — who do you figger to get to file on this place for you? Anybody that's got a right to file might want it themselves. Who is goin' to do said filin'?"

"My wife," replied King, and turned to Nancy Porterfield.

"Son-of-a-gun," rumbled Pack. "How much money have you got to start a ranch, anyhow?"

"Not enough," admitted King. "But what's the difference? It's a long life. And we're on our way. Here's the house. We always can butcher our meat. Plenty of firewood free. What else? Boys, I want you all to know I'm a fool for luck."

"Yeah," repeated MacGabriel. "I'm glad to get shut of you on my place. Never had a worse puncher." A thought occurred to him. He turned and whispered into old man Spring's ear. Spring nodded and likewise whispered to the adjoining cattleman. This sort of thing went on for quite a few minutes. "Make it three," suggested Dad Labadie.

"Why be a piker," put in Steve Pinchot,

153

another of that rancher group. "Make it five apiece."

"Done," agreed MacGabriel. "Does that go all around?"

King Merrick moved uneasily. "What are you idiots mumblin' about?"

MacGabriel cleared his throat. "You did yore part well, King. Now none of us wants to see you trampin' from door to door and beggin' bread. That sure would be a nuisance. Boy, we're makin' our weddin' present now. Five head of stock from each of us. That's thirty-five beeves. You earned it and Lord bless the both of you. A little cheer has come out of all this sorrowful mess."

There were tears in Nancy Porterfield's eyes. She gripped King's arm tighter and looked all around her proudly. King squared his shoulders. "I tell you, I'm just simply a fool for luck."

"That's right," was MacGabriel's retort. "I never had a worse ranch foreman."

THE KILLERS

Chapter One

One long, thin spiral of breakfast smoke rose from the cabin chimney and dissolved into the overcast sky of a November morning. The fine fall weather was behind and winter about to be announced in a squally burst of rain. Such at least was the glum prediction of Indigo, who squatted at the edge of the river, bathing cooking utensils in nature's own dish pan. Indigo despised this farfetched and misbegotten form of cleanliness, nor would he have endured it save that his partner Joe was a regular woman for housekeeping and even insisted on the ridiculous business of sweeping the cabin once a day. Rather than sweep, Indigo would have worn a circle around a pile of dirt.

But winter was coming. Deciding that the pots and pans were approximately sanitary, Indigo gathered them and started for the cabin, cocking a jaded eye to the gray heavens. The glint of warmth no longer lay on the river's surface as it swept past cabin and clearing; the dew hung lower in the hilly bowl that was their home. All along the pine slope across the river and away back up the canyon — where the river stormed its way through rugged shores — the shadows shifted and settled.

Indigo's bones ached. They ached in rheumatic sympathy with the impending dampness and they ached because he and Joe had labored drearily for a week bringing down the winter's supply of wood. Wood was piled on three sides of the cabin, wood was ricked against the barn, and the increasing accumulation of it stretched around the house like an Indian stockade. Never one to greet the dawn with a glad and joyous cry, Indigo stared at the monstrous monument to drudgery with a sour spirit. Joe seemed to figure life was going to be one long eternal winter from now on. And what were they, anyhow? Cowpunchers or loggers?

He went in and hung up the frying pan and the wet pots. Coming out again, he built himself a cigarette and sniffed the air. All told, Indigo weighed around a hundred and twenty pounds, including artillery and the umbrella-like sombrero he wore; a skinny little man with a peaked nose, a button-hole mouth and a pair of hazel eyes that turned green when he was angry. Suspicion of the world and a full knowledge of its many iniquities lay upon the smaller partner's face. He had red hair, he was a bundle of dynamite, and under his vest he concealed, like some terrible and criminal weakness, an absolutely dollar-sound heart.

"Goin' to rain like hell and gone in a minute," he muttered at Joe, now passing in with an armload of wood.

"Well, I guess we're about fixed for it," said Joe.

"I wouldn't wonder," jeered Indigo. "Not after cuttin' down enough timber to clear a road from here to Mexico."

Joe said nothing for the moment. He neatly arranged the wood in the box, saw the rivulets falling down the wall from the damp dishes, and came out to the porch. "You seem to dislike the touch o' water, don't you? Ever poison any of your family?"

"It has its uses and its handicaps," grunted Indigo and settled down on his hunkers. "I drink it with coffee and now and then I wash with it. It looks pretty, got no taste to speak about, and don't smell much. I can take it or leave it alone. Now you got my sentiments about water."

"Ahuh," drawled Joe, punching back the

lid of his hat. The first patter of rain struck across the bench but neither of them paid attention. It was a fixed habit of theirs to smoke a cigarette after meals and watch the lulling water go by. After years of drifting about the face of the West, these two strangely matched men had fallen in together, and now were holed up in their own cabin, on their own ground. The ever green hills faced them and the open desert lay just behind.

"Goin' to do our seedlin' peach trees a lot of good," reflected Joe, easing his long, symmetrical body over the steps. The slight trace of silver crusted his hair and wrinkles of shrewd wisdom sprayed the edges of his eyes. But the eyes themselves were blue and infinitely kind. He was a man who, having seen much evil and violence, still found the world fine and fresh.

"Say," demanded Indigo, "we'd ought to have fresh fruit on them trees next summer, huh?"

"No. Three-four years yet."

"You mean we got to sit here and watch the damn things grow up?" grunted Indigo. "I'd as soon buy my peaches from a store basket. And them's the trees we sunk better'n a month's wages in. What'd you git so many for?"

"Some might die, or blow over. Got to think of those things."

"Habit of yours — to think of everything. Then somethin' happens which ain't thought of. Never saw it fail." He turned to the wood. "And look at these mountains we done dragged off the hill. Like as not we'll mosey off somewheres and not come back till spring, and never use a stick of it. It ain't human and it ain't healthy to slave like a couple of goats."

"Which reminds me," drawled Joe, "we got to go into Smoky River town and stock up for winter. Oats, three-four hams to hang on the rafters, plenty of tobacco, a jug of liquor — and I'd sure like to find a box of apples in this wilderness to lay in."

"Must figure to die right here on the premises," growled Indigo.

Joe chuckled. "No sir. I aim to spend a good, comfortable winter. The first — and maybe the last — since I was a kid. I've figured on that for some years now, just sort of turnin' it over in my mind durin' the winters I rode range and the summers when I sweat. It's sort of growed on me — and here's where I cash in. Just like a winter when I was a young fella in Kansas. In a house with the snow heapin' up, eaves high and the wind howlin' acrost the plains. Warm fire burnin' in the stove. Something cookin' on the stove. Cellar full of grub, cider in the keg and the whole blamed family livin' in the kitchen. Dad mendin' harness, my mother toastin' apples for me. And I can remember like it was yesterday, goin' up to the attic at night to sleep. Wind batterin' right against my head and me sinkin' down into a feather mattress. My mother used to come up and tuck in the blankets."

The words broke off suddenly. The tall partner's eyes seemed to narrow into the distance and Indigo was again aware of that sadness underlying the big man's life. Presently Joe was speaking once more, but the genial humor had gone and there was nothing but slow, somber regret in his voice. "A man's nothing but a fool when he tries to bring back anything. What's gone is gone until the trumpet sounds — and I ain't so sure of it then. There won't be any more winters like when I was a kid. There won't be any more fine summers like when I was twenty and the world was before me. And when today is gone — "

Indigo moved uneasily and spoke with gruffness. "Well, don't cry about it. Gettin' damp enough around here. Say — listen. Hear that?"

The rain's patter increased swiftly. But

above it and above the rhythm of the river sounded the muffled detonation of shots. Irregular, dying, coming again. And then subsiding altogether. Indigo, whose hackles bristled at the first scent of trouble, wheeled and faced the bench behind the cabin. Joe only turned his head to listen better. And so they rested.

"Somebody else fixin' up for the winter. We better get our venison likewise."

"If that's a gent huntin'," prophesied Indigo, darkly, "I'm that other king o' France."

Joe chuckled. "Trouble with you is the milk o' human kindness in your system has clabbered. You want trouble. You'd spit in a grizzly's face right now to get action."

"Oh, I don't know — " began Indigo, and stopped. The both of them stood up and turned toward the bench, watching. Up there on the crest of the ridge a rider appeared, vague and shifting in the lowering darkness and screening rain. A horse shot down the slope in staggering spurts; the man swayed as if drunk, making no pretense at guidance. But when he reached the narrow alley between corral and wood piles he seemed to collect himself sufficiently to stiffen, make a course through the opening, and rein in at the porch. Then a strange thing happened. He looked down with haggard, fear-ridden eyes, cringed in the saddle and slid off on the right side of his mount, putting the beast between himself and the partners. A thick, desperate warning shot over the short interval.

"For God's sake, boys, get back out of range! Clear that corner and give me a chance! — I'm running for my life!" He sprang to the horse's head, twisting it desperately as if to use the beast for shelter. A shot's echo rolled down the slope, sodden and vicious; a furrow of clotted earth sprang up at the fugitive's feet, causing him to flinch. Indigo, with the flashing reaction of a veteran, had drawn without a sound and was firing at a blur on the ridge top. Another shot beat through the thickening rain and struck fairly. The fugitive threw his head back, teeth bared in a terrific spasm of agony, and staggered a few paces before falling in a huddle. Indigo swore violently and was in the fugitive's saddle at a leap, turning and slashing up the bench regardless of safety. Joe knew better than to waste his breath in warning; instead he did the only possible thing, which was to cover Indigo's blind attack. His long arm snaked inside the cabin door and came out grasping a rifle. He cleared the porch, cleared Indigo's path and pumped bullets against that dim strip where the ambusher had been a moment before. But the man was gone now, fading away almost before the echo of his shot had been whipped away by the wind. And the fugitive was gasping an incoherent sentence.

Joe wheeled. The man — no more than twenty-five — was dying. And though the silver-haired partner had seen a hundred untimely ends, he was never to forget the agony of despair in that white face feebly tipped to the rain. Whatever halting explanation the fugitive had already spoken was lost and beyond recovery; the knowledge of it seemed to dredge up one last layer of frenzied energy.

"Lonesome — Cowcamp — Lingard, it's black — " Then nothing more; nothing but a cruel gush of blood and the guttering out of another life, while the rain slashed down. Joe laid aside the rifle and bent thoughtfully over, testing the heartbeat. His lean lips tightened.

"Twenty-five years to make a man. One piece of lead to destroy him. Mortal man — the ruler of all things in the world but himself."

Lifting this dead youth to the partial shelter of the porch, he went inside for a tarpaulin to lay over the body. It was apparent to Joe's sharply exploring eyes that somewhere back along the hot trail the youth had dismounted to make a stand. Yellow mud caked his boots and also the front of his clothes, presumably where he had flattened himself against the earth in defense. Without a doubt he had fled in fear, stopped to make a vain fight, and fled again, until death had caught up with him.

Within the space of five minutes the shape of the world roundabout was twisted and blurred by the tremendous downpour. Water cascaded from the porch eaves like a sheet of glass and Indigo, returning, was drenched to the skin. He shook the brim of his hat and stared at Joe with a green glitter of wrath in his eyes. "That buzzard! He took for the timber along the rim of the canyon. Nor more'n a couple hundred yards ahead of me, but I couldn't see him in this weather and I ain't goin' to poke my head into no ambush. What're we goin' to do about it — sit by and twiddle fingers?"

"Whose quarrel is it?" murmured Joe, plunged in somber thoughts.

"When a gent comes on our property and bashes hell outa things, it sorta becomes our quarrel if you ask me," was Indigo's belligerent retort. "Find out anything?"

"The boy said something before he cashed in: 'Cowcamp — lonesome — it's black.' That's all."

"Cowcamp," repeated Indigo with aroused interest, "is the name of that tough town up at the northwest corner of the county. I dunno what he meant by 'lonesome,' nor that 'black' business, unless he meant the weather."

"So," mused Joe, shaking his head. "The trail he's taking is both lonesome and black. Maybe he meant that. But somehow I don't think a man, dyin' in agony and tryin' to get somethin' off his chest, would palaver about the weather."

"Look in his pockets," suggested Indigo, and bent to do it himself. But he found nothing else than a package of tobacco and a wadded bandanna soaked with blood. No marks of identification on his clothing, belt or gun. "His horse," said Indigo, peering at the weary animal, "has got a Running TM for brand. And say, he carried a rifle boot but no rifle. Now I wonder — "

"That shooting was undoubtedly between him and the gent that chased him," decided Joe. "See the yellow clay on his elbows? My guess is he made a stand for a little while, then dropped the gun and pounded the leather."

"Yellow clay?" Indigo's shrewish mouth puckered. "I don't recall no yellow clay in this neck of the woods. But I'd sure be interested to go find where it was."

"You'd also like to go right down to hell and look at the brimstone if you figured trouble was there," stated Joe.

"That's right — go ahead — try to make out I'm drummin' up grief!" exploded Indigo. "Put all the blame on my shoulders. Doggone it, Joe, there's somethin' rotten about this affair and you know it! If this boy was crooked, why did the other gent run away after he shot it out? Why didn't he come down and clear it up? I know why, you bet I do! It's because this lad tried to stick up for himself on an honest deal. Now if that ain't enough to make anybody boil over who's got somethin' else but ice in his veins — "

But he wisely held his words back. He knew his slow, easy-going partner very well, and understood perfectly the meaning of the settling, troubled glance Joe cast down at the dead youth. Joe was balancing up the scale of right and charity; struggling to prevent his heart from overwhelming his sense of caution.

"It ain't our fight," he said very slowly. "It's the sheriff's fight."

"Oh yeah," jeered Indigo. "Meanwhile the rain washes out the trail and that jasper is on his way. Uhuh, I know — "

A halloo floated across the river. Presently

a pair of men struck the ford and advanced down the bench to the cabin — two homesteaders known to the partners.

"Heard some shootin'," explained one. "So thought we'd ease in and see what — Who's that lyin' there?"

Indigo explained it tersely. "He come like a shot duck, was drilled by somebody from the ridge. Died quick, explainin' nothin'. Other gent vamoosed. Write your own ticket."

"I thought I heard shootin' away up — " began the homesteader, and was cut short by Joe who suddenly roused himself to action.

"Listen," grunted Joe, "one of you boys will have to stick here and the other ride to town for the sheriff and coroner. Indigo and me are goin' to backtrack and discover what makes folks so hostile thataway."

"It ain't our quarrel," said Indigo, sarcastically, but his skinny face brightened and he set off for the barn, leading the dead man's horse. He got back with a pair of saddled ponies before Joe came out of the cabin. "Better shift into somethin' dry, Indigo," he called through the door. The small partner went in, grumbling at the delay while the two homesteaders turned back the tarpaulin to study the dead man.

"Ain't I seen him someplace?" reflected one.

"Not me. Total stranger."

"Sure I've seen him. He's rode the upper hills now and then, lookin' for stray beef. Dunno the name, though."

Joe came out, covered head to foot with a yellow slicker and carrying a rifle in its boot, which he proceeded to lash under one saddle skirt. "We'll find out in Cowcamp," he told the homesteaders.

"Cowcamp? Damn little you'll find there. And the less you find the better it'll be for your state of health."

"Me," chimed in the other, "I'd hate to be caught dead around that sink hole."

Indigo waddled out, also skirted for the rain, and observed he had never yet found a town he couldn't ride into and out of. "Mebbe it's true I ain't always come out on the same side I went in, and mebbe it's also true I didn't tarry long. But these tough joints sort of interest me."

The partners swung up, slickers agleam with water. Joe called out a last order to the homesteaders. "One of you hit right for town. The other stick to the cabin and don't set the place on fire." Then side by side they quartered the slope, gaining the ridge, and swung along it toward the barrier of timber.

"Well," observed Indigo, pessimistically, "here's the beginning of that comfortable winter you spoke about. Ain't it just fine?" But he was quick to turn the subject after delivering this shot. "I wonder if that jasper is foolin' around those trees and waitin' for us?"

"Doubt it. He was in too big a hurry to depart. Here's his tracks, and the dead boy's tracks also." He reached for the rifle and laid it across the saddle, at the same time reining ahead of Indigo and entering the dark forest trail ahead of his partner. Nothing was said, but Indigo slackened his pace and gave Joe a twenty foot lead in order that both of them would not fall together into ambush. Joe kept his attention riveted on the gloomy vista ahead and on the hoof prints along the soggy underfooting, while Indigo watched the flanks and kept turning to sweep their rear.

So they pressed on, hearing the roar of Smoky River boom up from the canyon depths just to the left. The ranking pines broke the force of the roused wind, but the rain sluiced down in great liquid ropes and every trailing arm of underbrush spilled its load upon them. Once Joe paused to study some puzzling mark left upon the earth, then nodded and went somewhat faster. And eventually, after two hours of doubling and winding, they left the forest back of them and embarked upon the high desert. Heads braced against the slice of the elements, they galloped on.

"We're goin' to lose this trail pretty soon," called Joe. "Rain's about blotted it out now. But that fellow hasn't wasted any time and he don't seem to be afraid of being followed. He's linin' north straight as a string."

"Cowcamp ain't straight north," reflected Indigo. "It's west of north."

"Maybe this party's got other ideas. We'd better hustle along while the trail lasts."

The horses surged beneath them, running on into a sullen twilight; the rain made a curtain all around them. Here and there a blur along the trail came abreast and passed behind them without materializing. At the end of another hour a phantom shape stretched across their front and without warning they entered a rock barren through which the available footing darted left and right. They slackened their speed to cross it.

"Why ain't we explored this before?" demanded Indigo, plaintively. "Thought this damn country up here was all hills and trees."

"Got to save something for the last, I reckon."

"I don't like that statement," objected Indigo. "Sounds too much like an epitaph."

The trail of hoof prints had ended. And when, perhaps forty-five minutes later, they reached the far edge of the barren, there was nothing to guide them; no spoor, no landmarks. But Joe seemed to have made up his mind beforehand. He kept to the northerly course, resuming a stiff pace.

"What's on your mind?" asked Indigo.

"That fellow has been travelin' as straight as a honey-loaded bee all this while. Why should he change now? We'll work on that. Whoa, what's this doin' here?"

It was a river, appearing out of the mists unexpectedly; yellow with sediment and showing signs of roused turbulence. Perhaps in the summer it cut across the open desert as a yard-wide trickle, but at present it was rising rapidly and Joe, studying both the crumbling banks and the swift-flowing water, pursed his lips. "He didn't cross here, Indigo. Ain't exactly safe. We'll shoot along this side."

"You sure are doin' some fancy guessin'," grunted Indigo. "This can't be the same old Smoky that skims by our cabin."

"Nope. Guess the county's got an extra river to its credit."

"My mature opinion is," decided Indigo, trying to check a rivulet from skidding down his nose, "this country is too damn full o' water. We must be fifteen miles from home, ain't we?"

"Ahuh, and there's shelter not far off. Ketch the smell of smoke?"

The next instant they almost rammed a cabin squatting beside the river and half under a round knob of a hill. There was a light glimmering through a window and sparks reached the chimney top before being snuffed out. A corral and lean-to stood aside from the place and a solitary horse moved uneasily in the partial protection of the slanting roof.

"Better put our guns up before we hail that joint. Won't pay to scare anybody."

In silence they slid the rifles into the boots. Joe swept the whole place a second time — Indigo meanwhile unbuttoning his slicker to get some sort of play at his revolver — and then sent a long, casual hail across the distance. There was some delay before the door swung half open. A man peered into the flailing wind and rain; a man with a coal-black beard cut square at the end and a shock of equally black hair standing short and stiff from his scalp. His eyes were quite sharp, but seemingly not unfriendly. In his left hand he held a coffee pot, as if it had just been lifted from the stove.

"My gosh!" he bellowed. "Don't stand out

there waitin' on no etiquette. Put your horses in the shed and come in! It's awful damned miserable out."

"Thanks kindly," drawled Joe and led around to the shed. The man still held the door open for them when they returned on foot.

"Come right in. Coffee's right hot and I'll pour you a good stiff jolt."

Joe's apparently aimless glance absorbed three interesting facts. The man's cheeks and nose were whipped red from recent exposure, his clothes were damp from recent riding, and on his boots was a smear of that same yellow mud the dead man had been smeared with.

Chapter Two

Indigo's practiced eye had also observed these telltale marks. Going into the cabin first he walked toward the stove and thus, when the door closed, the bearded man was behind the partners. But his only reaction was to flash an inquiring glance from one to the other and then set the coffee pot back on the fire. To be boxed by strangers apparently did not trouble him at all. Giving them his broad back he rummaged around a cupboard for three tin cups and a can of condensed cream which he slid to the table, meanwhile talking with a cheerful unconcern.

"We had our cake, now we got to eat crusts. Fine summer, but it sure looks like a miserable winter. I'd hate to ride in this rain. Wouldn't ask a dog to go out. My theory is that water ain't healthy. Softens a fellow up — gives him rheumatism."

"Your sentiments are shared by my partner," said Joe and grinned. A wet rifle stood back of the stove, a wet hat lay on the floor. And some other party had been in the cabin very recently for there were two dirty dishes and two sets of knives and forks in a pan under the cupboard.

"Oh yeah?" grunted Indigo morosely. "Well, I ain't no duck."

"A man of wisdom," applauded the host and reached for the coffee pot. Indigo sat quite still and Joe knew by the slight stiffness of his partner's back that the latter was waiting for some break of disaster. But if Joe suspected treachery his lean and shrewd face did not mirror it. He took his coffee and drank with gusto. The host took a sip and peeled his coat, revealing belt and gun, at which Indigo very delicately balanced his cup in his left hand and appeared to be scratching his ribs with his free fingers.

"Makes a man hot," explained the bearded one. "I been bustin' around the prairie some this mornin', but from now on I hole up for the winter." The rest of the coffee vanished at one gulp and he tossed the empty cup into the pan of dirty dishes. "Don't tell me that you boys are goin' to travel far in this hell-slantin' storm. Make yourselves at home. Stick right here until she clears — if it takes all winter."

"That's kindly," observed Joe and rolled a smoke, "but we got a travelin' spell. What's north of here, anyhow? Any towns?"

"Strangers to these parts," countered the bearded gentleman, and permitted himself a full, prolonged stare at Joe. As affable as were his manners, Joe saw very little charity or sunlight behind those almost black pupils that were surrounded by curiously clay-colored rings.

"Total," agreed Joe, feeling Indigo's fretful look upon him. "Our territory is south about twenty-five miles. Comes a time, though, when folks get the itch to go see."

"There's a town eight miles on a slant yonder," said the bearded fellow, pointing one arm. "But it won't improve your education none as I can foretell."

"Without civic virtue, maybe?" drawled Joe, appearing to enjoy himself.

"You been hearin' jealous talk around Smoky River or Plaza San Felipe," accused the bearded one.

"Folks will gossip," stated Joe very gently and studied the trailing cigarette smoke. "You was speakin' of Cowcamp."

"It is some conservative in taste and opinion. Just a tight little place which likes to pick its own citizens."

"Ahuh — one big happy family," murmured Joe, at which the bearded one's eyes perceptibly hardened and narrowed. "And what," pursued Joe, "might be straight up the river?"

"A valley called Lonesome," said the man, flat and definite.

"Folks live in it?"

"Ye-es."

Indigo plainly had stood about all of this palaver he was able to. Catch-as-catch-can conversation he detested as fruitless. He was, moreover, boiling with some sort of an idea and kept turning a brightly suggestive eye on his partner. Joe refused to meet it and drawled softly on. "Funny name. How can a valley be lonesome with people in it?"

"Because that valley ain't the kind of a valley you might think a valley was," said the bearded one levelly.

"Well, if there's people in it my partner and me can ride on till dark comes and hole up comfortably. I reckon we had best saunter. This rain ain't goin' to get any better and it sure can't be worse."

"Was I you," commented the bearded gentleman without a chemical trace of emotion, "I'd leave the valley alone and quarter up the hill to Cowcamp."

"What's the catch in that?" Joe wanted to know.

The bearded man stared long and inscrutably at the tall partner before speaking. "I like you boys, cuss me if I don't. Wouldn't want any harm to come to either of you. We're peculiar in this country, but mostly we exercise our strange ways among ourselves. Speakin' of nobody in particular, what would be the percentage for anybody to dip his spoon in anybody else's coffee?"

"A deep thought," Joe acquiesced gravely. "Yes sir, a soul searchin' thought. But was that the reason?"

"Mebbe yes, mebbe no. The river's pretty high and it's a narrer, slippery trail into Lonesome. Awful easy for a man to lose his footin'. I've seen more than one gent float down this river on his way to the sea."

"Oh, hell," exploded Indigo, "I don't see no butter come from all this churnin'. Let's fork and drift."

"Not a bad idea at that," agreed Joe and opened the door. "Obliged for the shelter and the refreshments. Hope we meet again sometime. Be a pleasure."

"That depends on where the meetin' is," said their host. "I still think the trail into the valley is some ticklish, not to say downright dangerous. Let the remark lay awhile, then turn it over. In case you hit for Cowcamp and meet anybody curiously inclined, just

180

say you saw Clee Lingard — Black Clee Lingard."

Indigo flashed an emerald green glance at his partner, and the shrewish lips tightened down. But Joe nodded and herded his partner to the shed. Nothing more was said until they faced the rain again and the cabin became a blur behind. A flat stretch of country marched beside either bank of the stream and then tilted abruptly up into the pine slopes. The river cut its way between sheer shoulders, coming out of the cramped valley that lay compressed between the ridges.

"It's him," stated Indigo. "Not a doubt in the world he killed that boy."

"Yeah. At first I figured the boy might've meant it was growin' dark when he said 'it's black.' But what he tried to tell us was it was Black Clee Lingard. That makes sense. That dude with the pillow stuffin' on his chin killed the kid, plain as daylight. And I figure he knew we was onto the fact he did it. But was he touchy about it or nervous? Not a bit. Something all-fired queer there. Cowcamp and Lonesome, we know what they stand for, but what was the boy hintin' at when he strung the words together?"

"The answer is yonder," said Indigo, pointing through the rock shoulders into the hazy reaches of Lonesome Valley. They had arrived at a point where the trail broke two ways, one fork going beside the river into that undetermined land, the other curving leftward and high into the pines — Cowcamp bound. "It's there," added Indigo. "How about it?"

"I'm inclined to — "

A shot's echo came from behind and, in a moment, there was another. Joe's shrewd eyes raked the bluff tops with a suddenly roused interest. "I was inclined to agree," he went on. "But on second thought I guess we better hit for Cowcamp and let this valley alone today. We ain't wanted, that's certain. Those shots sounded like a signal and I'd be willin' to bet there's a gentleman up in those trees waitin' to knock us into the river when we try to go through. Lingard's warnin' was plain enough."

"The black-whiskered bastard," growled Indigo. "Nobody's goin' to tell me where I can't go!"

"Cowcamp first," insisted Joe. "Turn left and climb. Not ready to register on St. Peter's hotel book yet."

Indigo grumbled all the way along a mile climb that took them well into the ridge. At intervals they saw the thinning underbrush just short of foggy emptiness on the right, but they were not aware of Lonesome Valley's isolated and hemmed-in position until, at the end of a half hour, the trail veered from its straightness and led them to the very brink of a thousand foot slide. This seemed to be some sort of an observation post, for the trees had been cut away and the brush slashed to command a full view of all that lay below.

Perhaps a mile across was another ridge, and between the two ran the river. Meadow land lay up and down the left bank for about two miles, but was no wider than three hundred yards at any point between water and upslanting rock. Almost in the center of this flat expanse was a rambling house, a barn and several lesser buildings — all half hidden in the rain and fog.

"What's stretched between them houses?" asked Indigo.

"Wagons, farm implements, logs, baled hay — anything that might make a barricade," said Joe. "Looks like they've made runways from one place to another to keep from bein' shot. Nice country, Indigo."

"By gosh, if they ain't got sod on the house roof," muttered Indigo. "Now you can tie that? Afraid of fire, or bullets from above? Say, mebbe that's why this spot was cleared away — so a gent could lay here and fill that roof full of holes. If it ain't the *damnedest* thing I ever — "

"Indigo," broke in Joe excitedly, "take a good look at that valley. We're standing on one wall. Across is the other. We passed the lower mouth, which was the same as guarded. Now if you look ahead where the valley bends a little bit you'll see the ridges closin' in again and a sort of rapids in the river. Any way you look, it's locked up — in case anybody wanted to lock it up. There's all that protection down below. What's it mean? Either somebody is down there and can't get out, or somebody's up here and don't want nobody to get in."

"I see a little bird," grunted Indigo and let his gun hand rove downward. A coated figure moved suddenly out of the brush nearby and advanced on them with a cradled rifle. It was a rather young man with a peaked, hostile face.

"Ain't you got your bellyful of lookin'?" he challenged.

"Mebbe you look with your belly — I don't," snapped Indigo, ready to fight. But Joe, always the peacemaker, intervened with a soft question.

"This your private property?"

"Same as such."

"What's down there?"

"Runnin' TM outfit," was the man's surly reply.

The partners swapped glances. "You a Runnin' TM man?" pressed Joe.

"Me?" spat the man. "I'd rather be a woggle-eyed hop toad! Hell no! Don't you know nothin'?"

"Almost nothin'," drawled Joe, "but I always try to learn. Sometimes I don't get much help, like now. Any trail around here leadin' down?"

"If they was, you wouldn't use it," stated the fellow with heavy emphasis.

"Oh, I don't know about that," grunted Indigo. "You don't look so broad around the pants to me."

By way of answer, the man whistled softly, and directly two other men, unpleasantly glum, stepped from different parts of the damp thicket, guns raised. "Hard guys," explained stranger number one. "Guess they come from Bitter Creek where folks knock the rocks outa their drinkin' water." He swung on the partners. "I dunno where you buzzards come from, but start the hell back there sudden."

"You still don't look so fat in the britches," announced Indigo in a brittle singsong manner that announced the rising battle spirit.

Once more Joe soothed the situation. "Met a man down below who said I might mention his name. It was Lingard — Black Clee Lingard."

A change came over the hostile individual and guns dropped. "Why didn't you say that before. Where you goin'?"

"Cowcamp."

"Go on then. This country ain't safe to putter around. And for your information, I wouldn't show too much interest about Lonesome Valley when you git to Cowcamp. Folks might take offense."

"What I have to know," pursued Joe, "is what your interest in that valley is?"

"Let it ride," muttered the man. "And get goin'."

Indigo stared at the group with unmistakable meaning and was on the verge of launching one of his sweeping declarations when Joe reined into the trail and pushed Indigo's horse onward. Indigo's escaping wrath was like the steam blast of a boiler. "They'll live to eat that! They'll grovel in the dust before I'm through! Bunch o' gimlet-eyed, snake-hipped sand rats — givin' us the bum's rush! And you took it like the little Sunday school boy. I'm plumb surprised at you, Joe. Ain't it plain by now that all these highbinders is hooked up to that Clee Lingard? Furthermore, ain't it clear the dead fella rode a Runnin' TM horse — which is the outfit in that valley? These jaspers are tryin' to wipe out the TM — no less."

"Mebbe for good reason," Joe mused. "We don't know anything about this fight yet."

"There ain't any reason them sons o' bitches could have which would be good."

"Let the dew cool you off," suggested Joe in a different voice. The tall partner had put on a new manner and Indigo instantly recognized the explosive quality to it. Joe's eyes were fixed steadily ahead as they hastened through the pines, came out onto open soil and moved toward Cowcamp. His serene face was bereft of easy humor, the whole cast of jaw and mouth had grown rigid with inner feelings. It was still that way when the outline of a town broke the mists and they quartered upon it. Beside them was a square of land enclosed in a barbed-wire fence with many headboards rising up. A cemetery. Joe's attention was drawn to a fresh grave just inside the wire, and he drew over to it.

"This might help as a reason for warfare. It says: 'Jake Lingard, October 19th — ' That's five days old, Indigo."

"Damn country seems to be nothin' but Lingards. All them epitaphs got the same monicker. Seem to die frequent — which is no bad news to me."

"Here we go," muttered Joe. Side by side they entered the street end, the shadows of a short day flickering around them. Lights gleamed here and there and an occasional straggler breasted the rain. Turning into the mouth of a stable they dismounted and were met by the straight, cold inspection of a roustabout who had no word for them, civil or otherwise. They unsaddled. Joe, seldom allowing his temper to fray through, shifted on the roustabout with a startling swiftness. "What the hell are you standing there for? Get these animals settled and stalled. If you're tryin' to imitate an ossified mummy, it's a success. Now boost."

"Talk big," sneered the roustabout. "It won't last long."

Joe towered over the man, a crackle of wrath in his words. "It'll last just long enough for me to bust in that half-witted mug of yours. Get busy."

The roustabout led the horses back through the alleyway, muttering sibilantly. Indigo had to take three swift steps to catch up with the departing Joe, and as they tramped toward the lights of a restaurant farther along, the little man's cheeks straightened in worry. When the easy-going Joe got peevish the situation was indeed ticklish, and he voiced his apprehensions.

"Somethin' tells me, Joe, we took one step too many comin' here. I don't feel right. I feel like somebody's about to drop a rope on me."

"Yeah," admitted Joe. "You're right. We been followed every inch of the way from the hills. We're bein' watched right now. I wonder if we'll ever see our horses or gear again. We may get pushed to the wall. If we do — "

"Eat first and consider that afterwards," said Indigo in one of his rare moments of procrastination. "I'm so hollow they could use me for a bass drum."

The restaurant was empty save for a slatternly woman who poked their vittles ominously across the counter and then retired to a shaded corner to watch them with interest. Eating was a dreary chore to be finished quickly. Outside, they tarried a moment to build up their smokes. Then Joe wheeled with an air of swift finality. "Might as well get it over with. We're in a jam — a bad one, Indigo. I feel it creep right through my bones. Mark this street well in your mind, for in a little bit it'll be dark and I've got a hunch that when we come out of the saloon next time it'll be in a hurry. . . ."

They pushed through the saloon doors. A crowd of men lined the far walls, grouped in evident anticipation. Up at the bar Lingard

— Black Clee Lingard with a mask of fixed antagonism on his face — was posted. His fingers toyed with the massive chain slung across his chest; a rising flare shot from his eyes and a cold cutting phrase struck the partners squarely.

"Been waitin' for you two long-nosed Paul Prys. Now I got somethin' to say."

Chapter Three

"You cover a lot of ground in a little while," observed Joe, going forward. Indigo, within the compass of one glance, had numbered and assayed that room of people. He stalked stiffly to the bar and wigwagged his parched condition with a thumb. He drank, boosted the bottle to Joe and then leaned his back against the bar, thumbs hooked in his belt, eyes glimmering with an incredible green light. For a little while he looked into space, waiting for the retarded kick of his drink. His nose twitched, his wizened cheeks wrinkled up with long traverse lines and he began to stare from one individual to another; a direct, personal and unfriendly stare that contained a sort of reptilish and unwinking danger in it. And by degrees his dynamic spirit roused itself: Indigo was priming himself for conflict.

"You never got out of my sight," stated

Black Clee Lingard. "I saw you ram into my boys on the ridge. I saw you stop at the cemetery. Had you tried to turn and duck back into the trees on any part of that journey my bullets would have dropped you both."

"So we had a personally conducted tour?" drawled Joe. But Indigo, listening if not looking in his partner's direction, caught the tightness of that drawl and he knew what it meant. Very casually he shifted his little body and slid his right thumb farther back on his belt.

"I know who you are," went on Black Clee. "Why didn't you stay in your own country, stead of chasin' after me?"

"Not denyin' your part in that shootin' then?"

"Me? Hell, no. I killed that back-bitin' little fool. Trailed him twenty-five miles to do it and make no bones over the proposition. I run this country — which you're to soon discover. I'm askin' you again, what business you got hornin' in?"

"The fact is," stated Joe, "we're a little particular who dies in our yard."

"He was a Marshall, one of the Runnin' TM Marshalls. It was him that killed old Jake Lingard — you saw the grave."

"Any public reason?"

"The reason goes back many a year and will do you no good to know," grunted Black Clee. "Man for man, a killin' for a killin'. And when the swappin' is all done they'll be no Marshalls left. This is a Lingard town — a Lingard county. When we're through starvin' and pinchin' the Marshalls, it'll be a Lingard Lonesome valley. I give you fair warnin' to keep your skirts clear. I took you for men of mature judgment; I made my meaning crystal clear. Since you elected to throw in with the other side, it's your grief."

"What makes you think we have?" challenged Joe very softly. Indigo sighed and took one small step along the bar, clearing Joe and getting nearer the door. The barkeep leaned over and whispered meaningly, "Don't get the fidgets, brother. You ain't goin' any place."

"If a man ain't for the Lingards, he's against them," said Black Clee. "No neutrals and no innocent spectators. Quick or dead. I give you warning. You figgered to make some wild play, but it don't go. I'm crimpin' your deck of cards right here and now. There's too much in the atmosphere tonight to let you roam loose. When we're finished with the main business we'll hold court on you. That's my talk, and my talk goes."

"Maybe, maybe not," mused Indigo, tipping his head slightly. Indigo's brow creased with sudden concentration. He was trying to figure some way of horsing the barkeep — who stood at a bad angle — out of ensuing play that was coming as sure as death and taxes. Joe's head was up. That was ample signal. And Joe would take care of Black Clee, depending on Indigo for the rest.

"No maybe — " began Black Clee, and was suddenly diverted by the entrance of three new men dripping wet. One of them came toward the bar, speaking.

"Before we throw the horses into the stable, Clee, do you want anything else?"

"Other boys relieve you all right?"

"Ahuh."

"Get your supper and be ready to ride again."

"A little drink will do no harm," said the spokesman, at which all three broached the bar, between Indigo and Joe, and solemnly poured. This was worse yet. They had Joe front and rear; but Indigo's flickering attention, spreading out to a number of things at once, saw the nearest gentleman's gun butt within the pluck of his arm. Horses outside — and the bulk of the loitering gentlemen on the opposite side of the room would never dare fire at the bar. These thoughts flashed in quick succession, touched the dry powder in Indigo's brain and produced an instant explosion. He cleared his throat, yelled, smashed for his gun, and wrenched violently at that butt exposed to him. He saw Joe's hat make a circle and by that signal knew his partner had not been caught napping.

After that he had no time to look. The nearest rider, bereft of his piece, lurched about and found its round, cold maw set against him; it was not that, however, which caused him to pull back and catch his breath; rather it was the shock of what he saw in Indigo's glittering green eyes — the promise of death ready to leap at him. Pallor erased the wind-whipped red of his cheeks and he forced himself against the bar.

The barkeep elected to gamble it out. His arms swooped below the mahogany surface; then a full-throated bellow pitched out of his chest and sheared to a scream. Indigo's first gun swung and a bullet cracked the man in the chest, sending him down and out of sight in the litter of bottles and kegs. "Flippers up high — quick!" snapped Indigo, singsonging the words. The two remaining riders obeyed without further hesitation, were stripped of their guns and left alone.

Indigo stepped to the rear, cat-like, until

he had his back to the street wall of the saloon and could better command the crowd at the far side of the place. Nobody over there had dared to shoot, and now the chance had passed by, for Indigo's guns roved from party to party and the tide had turned. Joe's deceptive drawl, quiet and effortless, reached every corner of the room.

"I know you boys are hard and downright mean. You told me so yourself. But I reckon we can all take lessons once in a while. Here's yours, and many happy returns of the day. Lingard, keep in front of me and step sidewise to the door."

Indigo drew a deep breath and relaxed, at the same time feeling a glow of pride. Joe had a way of drawing the sting and the poison out of such a tight situation with just such lazy talk; it had more effect than a posse of men. Venturing to look away for a second from the crowd, he observed that Joe's gun commanded Black Clee Lingard. The clan chief's body screened Joe, and on order slowly sidled toward the door. Indigo had seen many a black and unfriendly face but never one more swollen with murdering rage than Black Clee's at this moment.

"You will never live to ride free from Cowcamp," said Black Clee, the words trembling under the pressure of that terrific temper. "You never will. Or if you do, you will never ride alive from this district! I rode twenty-five miles to kill that Marshall. I will ride twenty-five hundred to plant *you* — hear that! If it takes every man I got and the rest o' my life, I'll do it!"

But Joe only smiled in that tight, suppressed manner of his and bobbed his head at Indigo. "Peek out of the door and see if them horses is in front. Keep your eyes peeled for trouble."

Indigo shoved himself partly through the swinging doors. The three horses were at the rack, nobody moved abroad, but he saw the stable hand lounging within the shelter across the street. He reported all this laconically. "Set to ride, Joe."

"Go out first."

Another moment filled with dynamite. The members of the crowd had frozen and there was an oppressive expectancy in the saloon's sultry atmosphere. They were all waiting for the break to come, all poised for the swiftly approaching climax. Black Clee moved sluggishly under the impulse of Joe's gun, but his self-command had returned to him and once more he kept his face turned to his captor with an inscrutable expression.

Indigo went out, assuming a casual air for the stable hand who was plainly watching, and walked to the horses. It was growing quite black beyond the town and the rain's violence had increased. Joe was still inside, which worried Indigo; yet, shrewd and weathered in the ways of violence, he got a good grip on the trailing reins of the animals, to prevent their stampede in case of gun play, and put himself in a position to mount.

"Quit fiddlin' with them brutes," warned the stable hand. "Git away from there!"

Joe's tall and slim back appeared in the saloon doorway. Indigo was in his saddle like a flash and turned about with his gun on the stable hand never saying a word. The man stiffened and seemed ready to bolt at first chance. Joe had pulled Black Clee to a position in the doorway and stopped him there. "Now stand pat," the tall partner was drawling. "You're framed like a picture. I'd like to take you along with us to pass the dreary hours, but I reckon we'll meet again anyhow. Until then, be good." And with that he was up and beside Indigo and murmuring, "To the left, all the way around town. Let's go!"

They wheeled, bunched and raced on. The stable hand and Black Clee disappeared simultaneously. A riot of sound poured from the saloon and there was a man running across the street directly in front of them, firing at every stride, the flame buds blurred in the sheeting rain. Indigo took to cursing in round-bodied epithets, slicing the lead at this fellow. He staggered and fell as they spurred past into the deeper protection of the night.

The last building on the street was abreast. Joe veered to the right to skirt it and in doing so exposed his horse broadside to the street. A bullet ripped off the street — from the man presumably out of combat — and struck the horse in the barrel; he trembled, his front feet buckled and Joe, riding loose, was flung far over to the ground.

At once the town seemed crowded with men. They were in the street, ducking from alley to door; they were hurrying down behind the buildings, across back lots, and taking stations here and there in sprawling sheds set apart; they were racing for the stable to mount up and extend this chase, and they were even climbing to second-story porch roofs. Above the vigor of the wind and rain Indigo heard Black Clee Lingard calling from the stable, calling for his men to draw in. And a group of some size was beating directly toward them through the rear darkness of Cowcamp.

He had checked his horse instantly and

even then overran the capsized Joe. Wheeling back he called anxiously: "Joe — hurt? Where are you? Sing out — sing out?"

Joe was up and beside him. "Should have taken that third animal for somethin' like this. I'm comin' aboard. All right. Now get out of here before they set us afoot entire."

The pony, with a long day's riding already behind him, answered slowly to the double burden. Those men in the back lots were not more than fifty feet away, voices without substance in the dismally dripping night. Indigo was swearing again, applying the spur. They shot past the immediate point of danger and out of Cowcamp. In another one hundred yards the lights died away and they were lost in the cloaked immensity of the prairie.

"This goat ain't goin' to carry us no place in a hurry," was Indigo's gloomy prediction.

"Swing wide to the left and sink the spur for ten minutes more," ordered Joe. "They'll be saddled and out huntin' for us in another three minutes. We got to clear this district quick. After that we'll walk if it comes to the worst."

"You said so, not me," was Indigo's gloomy retort. The heat of the battle having left him, he was once more morose and foreboding. "I never got the walkin' habit and I'm too old a duck to learn now. That damn bartender didn't have no more sense than a jackrabbit! They'll rake this country with a comb. You and me — we got to watch our step. That Lingard buzzard'll do just what he said he'd do."

"Correct. Dab your spur again. We're not makin' any time."

"But I pulled a trick this night which I wouldn't of believed if somebody had told me. Lifted a man's gun outa his holster — lifted it cold and nothin' to go on. I tell you, Joe, we was in a tight pinch."

"In one yet. Rein in and sit quiet."

The drum of Lingard's bunch sounded up, rapidly strengthening and apparently headed right at them. Indigo twitched the reins and the partners sat motionless in the downpour. Of a sudden the pursuing men were abreast of them about a hundred yards to the right, marked by the swift pounding of their horses; then distance and the elements swallowed them.

Joe pondered. "Cuttin' tracks across the desert, hopin' to strike us. I bet they come back. But which way? More to the left or more to the right? We'll compromise. Head over there about where they passed. Lightnin' can't hit same twice."

"Say," inquired Indigo, "where we headed for?"

"The next stop is Lonesome Valley. We're payin' the Marshall outfit a visit."

"A hound for punishment, ain't you?" grumbled Indigo.

"Who suggested this vacation, anyhow? If you want to pull stakes for home — "

"I didn't say that, did I?" snapped Indigo. "I was just remarkin' you took your punishment in large and continuous doses. We got fine prospects of bein' picked off the trail in them trees. But if we get by — what about the Marshalls? Don't expect 'em to throw open the doors and kiss us."

"The way of the peacemaker is hard," opined Joe. "Hold everything."

Lingard's men came swooping down out of the thick weather again, driving by on their flank; vanishing, and strangely coming into hearing almost immediately thereafter on the right. The swift drum of hoofs abated and was lost.

"Just feelin' around — up to some sort of hell," whispered Joe. "Go ahead."

Indigo walked the jaded horse onward. A quarter hour, a half hour. Saying nothing, hearing nothing but the gusty wallowing of the wind and the strike of the rain. Lingard's party was lost to them. By degrees the glow of supper and the heat of the recent fray had worn away and Indigo was stone cold.

His bones were knocking together shamefully and his aversion to water assumed monstrous proportions.

"Swing a little right," murmured Joe.

"Main trail into the hills?"

"Ahuh."

"Watch out. They'll be expectin' us to head home thataway."

"Ahuh. A little more right. Push the horse. We won't burden it much longer."

For another hour this dismal journey dragged on. Once they stopped, to catch a dim and wavering reverberation nearby. Still later Joe slipped to the ground and put his ear vainly to the prairie. If anything, the shadows piled thicker in front of them, and then they were confronted by rising ground and the straggling outline of timber. Indigo reined the horse at right angles to their former trail and skirted these trees, feeling for a break that would mark the trail. Joe grunted almost soundlessly. They stopped, the tall partner disappearing in the murk for ten long minutes, leaving Indigo a miserable and glum figure in the saddle. Presently Joe reappeared. "Take off the gear, save the rope and gun, and turn the horse loose. We walk a piece."

"This," stated Indigo, "is the last time I ever monkey in somebody else's quarrel."

All he had for an answer was Joe's soft chuckle. They struck up the trail and the trees took them into a blank, abysmal and dripping darkness. Joe was ahead and his land legs set a pace that in a little while had the sawed-off Indigo grunting. But there was no let-up and the little man's pride would not allow him to complain.

Joe's arm swept him off the trail. A rider came questing down out of the mist and passed, near enough for both of them to catch the smell of rain steaming against the horse's flanks. It was only a moment's rest, for Joe seemed to be bitten by the need for haste and plowed on. The trail grew stiffer, turned and became a level runway at the end of which they saw a tawny pulsing of light. Indigo muttered a brief warning and again they were off the trail, letting the night rider return past them. Abreast the horse shied away; a sullen voice carried down.

"Do that again, you hammer-headed son o' sin and I'll mash your ears into your neck! What's eatin' you? I'll — "

He pursued the trail and became a dim silhouette against the rising light. Joe followed, seeming to abandon all thought of caution. Another short bend brought them to a halt; twenty yards along was a wisp of fire that guttered and leaped to every fitful blast. Once a man cautiously appeared, poked fresh wood on the flames and then drew out of the light.

"That's the jump-off," muttered Joe. "Runnin' TM houses are below."

"A thousand feet below," added Indigo. "Now don't tell me — "

"That's right. We're climbin' off the cliff here. Come on."

They smashed into the brush, just short of being discovered and ridden down. A whole line of horsemen came along the trail from Cowcamp direction, turned the bend and halted a respectful distance from the fire. Joe tallied twenty men in the party and swore. "They mean to attack tonight. You and me have got to get down there."

"Well, if I got to be shot I'd just as soon be shot by a Marshall as a Lingard. What made me think we had any business in this in the first place?"

He trailed Joe gingerly. Ten yards brought them to the abrupt downcurve of the bluff's face. Nothing but a blank and flimsy fog lay before them, nothing but the quick striking stealth of hunted men lay at the end of their journey, if indeed they descended without breaking their necks. And still Indigo kept his own counsel and watched Joe's torso sinking below the brow.

"Good footing. Come ahead."

Rock rubble, a patch of brush, a few twisted logs and now and then a stubborn pine clinging to life — such was the ground below. Joe disappeared momentarily and when Indigo had skinned down the first sharp drop he heard his partner calling from another quarter. "Easier here. Come ahead. No time to lose."

"If you're in such an all-fired hurry," mumbled Indigo, "just let go and fall. Damn it, I been playin' duck all day and now I got to turn goat. What I really am is a jackass. What a life."

He fell into a rock pit awash with water, clawed through hazel and found himself hanging to a ledge that seemed to have no bottom. By infinitely painful degrees he worked over to solid ground. He had no idea where Joe was, no idea where anything was except Black Clee's gang. Looking up he saw the outlaw fire leaping to the sky in a great ragged spiral.

"Joe — where the hell — "

A fragment of his partner's voice whipped back from the depths. "Come ahead. Easier going here."

Everything cracked and groaned under the impetus of the driving elements. A fine night for the Lingards to attack. "I hope," swore

206

Indigo, "they all bust their damn necks." He hoped Joe knew where this outlandish and scrabbling pathway would lead them; as for himself, he could see nothing at all to indicate the habitation of man. It was as black as the grave and much more uncertain, and even the silvered surface of the river was buried beyond the rain fog.

In front of them were the beleaguered Marshalls who would undoubtedly shoot at the least stray sound, and behind them were the Lingards, probably now advancing to attack. So they were whipsawed, and all the while they climbed down this crazy slope, wet clear through to God's underwear. Not that Indigo was averse to battle. In his more candid moments he willingly confessed a liking for occasional trouble. But to toil like a couple of galley slaves to put themselves in a worse situation was piling it on a bit thick. Mumbling and muttering like a lost soul, he scraped his scrawny hide on the cracked edge of a rock and suddenly found Joe's thin shadow cleaving the greater darkness in front of him.

"We're here," whispered Joe.

"Yeah. And where are we? I tell you flat, I'll starve, die and rot down here afore I climb that slope. Of all the fool things a couple of fools could do in a fool universe — "

"The barn's just to the right. We just

missed piling into that barricade. Beyond the barn's the house. See that little crack of light?"

Indigo peered at the dim slice of yellow radiance that escaped through a boarded window. The barn, nearer at hand, loomed vaguely over them — at which he was seized by premonitions of danger. "Bet a cookie they've got an outpost in there. You and me had better drift away. Now that we're here, what of it?"

"Got to work fast," grunted Joe. "Lingards ain't far away. No place for innocent by-standers."

"I thought of that a long time ago."

"Come ahead."

Joe slid off. Indigo dragged himself wearily after, casting an ominous glance at the barn. The meadow land was soft and slushy with the torrential downpour and presently they were ankle deep in the overflow of the river. Joe had turned and was going parallel with the line of buildings, thus approaching the front of the main house by respectful degrees. A wagon suddenly barred their pathway, at which both partners stopped dead and stood motionless. At this point Indigo, born to defy all manner of traps, took the initiative and walked on to inspect the vehicle.

"All right," he reported.

"Stand behind it. I'm callin' the house."

"Which is goin' to prove interestin'."

The tall partner's ringing halloo beat through the rain and was met by utter silence from the dwelling. But they both saw a point of light shift from one barred window to another. Joe challenged again. And without ceremony a reply came cutting across from some refuge between house and barn. "Who is it?"

"Two friends of yours," answered Joe.

"Yeah. Likely. How the hell did you get in here if you was friends of ours: Snap an answer afore we blow you plumb down to the pit!"

"A young fellow bearing the Marshall name was shot this mornin' right by our clearin' on Smoky River, twenty-five miles below. What he told us was sort of interesting, so we come to dab a loop."

A longer silence. Some signal passed between house and barn, some shifting of forces occurred. Then another man's voice, flat and brittle, struck at the partners. "Come up here, you two! If it's more'n two we shoot without warnin'. I don't need to tell you to keep your hands high and your movements simple. Come on."

The partners fell side by side and trudged toward the voice, somewhere to the right of the house. Halfway Joe lifted his arms and Indigo copied with a grumble of protest. "Always makes me feel silly to do this. Hope those gents ain't nervous fingered."

The barricade broke through the dark and they were commanded by the still unseen individual to turn left and aim for the house. This brought them on a walk that scooted downward to the sod wings of a basement door. It stood open and they passed through. It slammed behind them and a voice muttered, "All right, Abe," and a lamplight sprang up to dazzle their eyes. In this basement, as vast as the length and breadth of the house itself, were many bunks, a stove, tables, and a rack of rifles glistening with oil. Nine or ten men made a ring around the partners.

Out of the group stepped a gaunt and weathered veteran as tall as Joe but older and grimmer and wearier; his eyes had the strength of steel in them and his lips were pressed in a thin line, severe — the kind of a mouth made by hardship or stubbornness. In absolute silence he studied the partners, his glance passing slowly from detail to detail, missing nothing, weighing everything. Indigo, always impatient under such circumstances, grew restless, but Joe calmly made his own reckoning of the crowd and immediately made up his mind.

"They ain't got the Lingard stamp on 'em," muttered someone.

"No. But what does that mean? Lingard buys help sometimes."

The old man raised a hand abruptly and the talking ceased. "Anybody ever see these fellows afore?"

Nobody spoke. It was evident that the Marshalls trusted nobody outside of their clan. Suspicion lay openly on every face. The old man ducked his head at Joe. "Tell your story — and tell it straight. May be you're friendly, but if you ain't our style of treatment allows for no quibblin'. We take our cue from the killers on the bluff."

"Not much time to waste," drawled Joe. "I already said one of your men was shot right at the doorstep of our cabin on the Smoky this mornin'. He mentioned two-three words which interested us to the extent we saddled and took the trail of the gent that had done the shootin'. Which brought us to the mouth of this valley and a cabin with the aforesaid gent in it. In due time it also brought us to Cowcamp, which wasn't friendly, and we got out by the skin of our teeth and decided we'd pay you a visit. My partner and me have been known to dally in a quarrel if it seems unequal."

"You saw my nephew, Jason Marshall," said the old man. "Out to stir up help. So they chased him as far as Smoky? How is he?"

"He's dead," said Joe briefly.

Nothing but an increasing tension and strain in the faces about him marked this piece of news. The old man spoke again, all emotion filtered out of his words. "I wrote that on the page afore he started, but he would go. And who was the killer?"

"I wouldn't say, except the gentleman admitted it openly. Black Clee Lingard."

"Another Marshall to his credit," breathed the old man and turned aside and ducked his head at one of the crowd. "Go upstairs and tell *them*."

"I said there wasn't any time to waste," stated Joe. "You will maybe have observed the big fire on the bluff?"

"Thirty-seven nights and days we've seen it," replied the old man and couldn't keep the sag of weariness out of his speech. "It don't never go out. But when a Marshall's killed it gets brighter. Which was why we knew Jason was dead afore you told us. Burnin' high for Jason tonight."

"Burnin' high because the whole damned Lingard outfit's up there," countered Joe. "They're stormin' you boys this evenin'."

And still they remained like statues. Neither the news of sudden death nor the threat of disaster moved them. They were calloused to shock, accustomed to tragedy; the expectancy of ill-fortune was in that room, heavy as the rain fog outside, and suddenly Joe felt a strange pity for them. His fine, serene face tightened. "How many boys you got in this fort — "

A short choked scream echoed from the upper part of the house, knife-like in its effect. It struck Joe; it broke into the reserve of these ten haggard defenders who stood in the basement gloom. The old man's arm lifted above his head with an abrupt gesture and a gleam of stubborn fire poured out.

"What was that?" challenged Joe.

"Jason's maw. It don't sound nice to you, does it? How would you like to've heard that scream four times in thirty-seven days? Death wail for that many Marshalls. Friend, if they's such a thing as hell on earth, here it is."

The partners exchanged glances. Indigo, whose fighting instincts flamed at the first sight of an underdog, had forgotten the misery of the weather and the humiliation of turning pedestrian; had forgotten everything but the stark fact that here was a quarrel in which his sympathies were fixed. The blue-green

213

eyes blinked knowingly at Joe and the tall partner swung around the circle of men, challenging them.

In such a situation as this there always came a time when the persuasive, latent leadership of this calm, silver-templed man began to be felt. It was not so much what he said or what he did; it was rather the very sight of him standing there, so sure and contained and quietly confident. He was a cool head, of that there could be no mistake; he was a fighter, an old hand at an old, old game. But more than that he was a man's man and the kind, shrewd simplicity of his nature was something never to be forgotten nor mistaken once it was felt.

Thus in this dead silent cell, ridden with unspoken despair, the alchemy of Joe Breedlove's will again manifested itself as it had along the trail of his past. Indigo had seen such a shifting of power to those broad shoulders before, but he never ceased to marvel at it and now, preoccupied as he was with the immediate strategy, he felt a proud stiffening of his own spirit.

Joe's softly slurring voice broke the spell. "If I was you, I'd post a few boys in your barn, and on the other angle of this house."

The old veteran lifted a head that meanwhile had fallen against his chest in brooding reflection. He pointed silently around the crowd and men moved away. Then his lulled suspicion woke afresh. "I don't know you."

"You will before this is done with," murmured Joe. "And if I was you I'd bring the womenfolk down here. This is my partner, Indigo Bower, and don't be misled by his size. He carries more dynamite in him than a powder house. My name's Breedlove. Where we come from doesn't matter and where we're goin' is immaterial since nobody knows and least of all, us. If it sounds strange to you that we should be hornin' in, just mark it down we're a couple of broken down hands with a dislike of rustin' away."

"Thirty-seven days," muttered the old man. "We're short of ammunition, we're down to our last beef and our horse stock is starvin' in the barn. Was we just men alone we could cut and run. Havin' women makes it different. Partner, you have picked up a losin' hand of cards. My name is Broderick Marshall of the Runnin' TM — which was, but pretty soon won't be."

Indigo tramped nervously about the gloomy basement. For all anybody knew the Lingard bunch might be right on top of them at this moment. It was high time to be up and doing, yet Joe, as was his habit, dallied as if no such thing as a fight was on his mind.

"What," asked the tall partner, "is behind these thirty-seven days of ruction, anyhow?"

"It goes way back," said Broderick Marshall. "Man is born to fight and the Lingards like fightin' better than most. An overbearin' set of people. What they see they want. Which applies to Lonesome Valley. A killin' started this war afresh. Jason got sucked into a play and had to knock over one of their men. They'd figgered it to be another Marshall out, but he was faster than they figgered. They're born killers. I reckon we're all killers now, but the Marshalls never liked to fight and would pay any price but one to have peace."

"What's that price?" demanded Joe, suddenly interested.

"Black Clee wants to marry one o' our women. Fact that she don't want him cuts no ice with him."

Joe's expressive face became shadowed and Indigo grunted, "The louse. Ain't he even human?"

"Killers — all Lingards," said Broderick Marshall.

A shot burst through the tension of that rain swept night and there was a running of feet overhead. Then a sudden, ragged volley beat against the Marshall stronghold and a high, angry cry marked the beginning of the assault. Joe sprang to action. "Two-three more boys outside. Rest of us upstairs! Waste no shots. We can't stop 'em from overrunning this clearing. Got to wait till they break through to sight. Women downstairs. Come on!"

Chapter Four

Indigo was up the stairs in four hurdling jumps, yelling, "They'll try the back side first, watch it close!" Then the women were hurrying down, seven of them, trooping the children ahead. Joe drummed crisp orders around the basement, all unconscious of the fact that he was taking over this battle as if it were his own. "I wouldn't put any more boys outside now, Marshall. How many in that barn?"

"Four."

"That's enough unless the fightin' switches over yonder pretty strong. Keep a couple at the basement door. Rest follow me up. Let them do the movin' around." He swung up the stairs, in time to catch a bronze-haired woman tripping on a middle step. His long arm cradled her fall and for a moment he felt the tight pressure of her hands gripping him. The faint fragrance of perfume was in her clothing; dark eyes — clear and unafraid — looked straight into his face a long interval and dropped away. A slow, soft "thank you" just reached his ears. Joe never knew what his answer was, for his mind was caught in conflicting swirls of thought and his attention raced a dozen separate ways.

The firing of the Lingards had increased; they were closing in and it seemed as if their attention was fixed upon the house, judging from the spat and impact of the slugs boring into the wood. He raced up the stairs with the rest of the Marshalls at his heels. Indigo had whipped out all but one lamp and was now crouching by a blanketed window, head thrust out it.

"Two of you boys on up to the second floor," ordered Joe. "If they try the porch, sling down on 'em, but never let a bullet go unless you know it'll hit something. That leaves five of us here. Enough. See anything, Indigo?"

Indigo's answer was a swift bunching of shoulders and a single shot into the ridden night. "Winged the — " and the rest of it came back in smoky, taut syllables. The blanket shook violently and Indigo sprang aside. "Down on your hunkers!" Bullets made a ragged pattern on the opposite wall. Lingard's men were curving about the house, commanding all its angles and slinging lead with a wild, reckless savagery.

"Let 'em waste it," observed Joe, grimly. "Sooner over. But they mean business."

Broderick Marshall knelt beside a divan with his head bowed. He seemed to be praying but Joe's remark roused him to a dull, dispirited answer. "A Lingard was born to fight. Nothin' stops 'em till they're dead. I have worn out the best part of my life buckin' 'em. And for thirty-seven days they've put the screws on us. It won't last much longer now."

"Stop that!" snapped Indigo. "I've climbed outa worse holes than this! Quit tattin' and go to fightin'."

"I've seen too many die," droned Broderick Marshall. "Well, hell's afire, we die when we die and that's all there's about it."

"True facts," assented Joe and took three wide steps aside. "Here we come!"

Some solid object struck the door a mighty blow. A panel screamed and splintered; elsewhere in the room glass jangled; and on the porch many feet tramped and dragged rapidly. "Blow the light, Indigo! Everybody stand aside. Let them come!"

Another mauling impact wrenched the hinges aside. The door slammed to the floor; buds of flame flickered on the porch, like monstrous fireflies, and lead spattered the room from corner to corner. Joe saw a figure weave dimly across the opening and he flung his first bullet that way. The shadow of the man dissolved into the earth. Then there was a plunging body coming through a corner window, and simultaneously more attackers poured through the doorway. The room was a furnace of fury, blasting waves of sound colliding and the very foundation timbers seeming to quiver.

Nothing but the madness of men could bring about so fantastic a scene; nothing but the fury of a killer tribe fed on tales of hate and nursing them like religious relics through the years. They stumbled and fell. They came on, pushed by the unreason of the night. One Lingard, turning out of the path of fire, collided against Joe and ripped his arms up to get a free play; Joe had seen that shadow bearing down and the barrel of his gun rose and descended. The man collapsed with a belch of wind. Elsewhere a vicious fight sent chairs and furniture reeling. Indigo's whoop of battle quivered mightily and sheared off. A voice summoned the Lingards outside and the gunplay began to climax upon the barn.

Suddenly the room was silent save for the irregular breathing of men. Joe broke the lull. "Indigo?"

"Yeah — still alive and sorry for it. Damn what a wallop I done took. But I poled the gent down. He's layin' across my boots this minute."

"Marshall — any of you boys hurt?"

"All right."

"All right here. Who's that rollin' on the floor?"

"A Lingard!" exclaimed Broderick Marshall, voice shaking.

Joe reached down and unbuckled the gun belt of the man huddled at his feet. Then he stepped over and performed the same chore with a second Lingard, who rolled slowly from side to side, murmuring: "I'm played out. Got no gun — lost it. I'm givin' in. You got me in the shoulder." Joe's fingers went exploring in the dark and came away. All the while his ears were tuned to the shift of the fight out by the barn. Another sound arrested his attention, a soft and irregular slushing of horses' hoofs from down the little valley.

"We've got to take a hand out yonder," he decided. "Any shotguns, Marshall?"

"Couple — three."

"All right. In the basement? Come along, Indigo. You other boys stick here and watch for another break this way. Keep these three buzzards on the floor humble." He ran down the stairs with Indigo behind him and stopped at the gun rack. "You take that double-barreled brute and I'll take this. Here's a handful of shells. We're goin' out this door and sting 'em some. Horses coming from the mouth of this valley. Either it's more Lingards or it's their own saddle horses bein' brought roundabout so they won't have to climb the slope."

Tarrying an instant at the basement door, he saw what a terrible pressure and misery this savage night put upon the women. They were huddled behind the protecting angles of the foundations, holding the children tight to their skirts, watching him with an indescribably haunting look. All but the woman with the bronze hair that gleamed like copper even in the dimming lamplight. She stood a few feet from the door, erect, graven-faced. One hand lay quietly across her breast and her fine, clear face was turned on Joe, missing nothing he did, catching every turn of his own countenance. And when he slid beside the door guards and lifted the two-by-four barrier he heard once more the low cadence of her voice.

"Be careful."

It might have been addressed to any of them, only Joe felt the strike of her glance and the sure knowledge that she spoke to him. He nodded, pulled the door slightly ajar and slipped out, Indigo cat-footing right at his rear. They tarried an instant to sweep the rising runway and then went up and reached the protection of an overturned wagon box. Lingard's men were a hundred feet beyond, girdling the barn and attempting to carry it. The flame points wavered and were blurred in the rain; and now and then a strong yell came vibrating back. A ram struck the barn and the shallow booming echo rose above the guns and storm alike.

"Tryin' to get in and set the hay afire," muttered Joe. "Let's crawl up and let 'em feel this BB shot."

"Don't they never get tired of fightin'?" grunted Indigo.

They left the runway and the immediate vicinity of the blockade for fear of ambush. Skirting behind it a distance, they closed upon the barn and again crept forward to the precarious protection of a shed. The distance between shed and barn was perhaps forty feet, and they faced the side of the large structure which contained the rear door. It was here that a half dozen Lingard men were battering a way inside. Joe murmured softly, "I'll open up, and then you follow and give me a chance to reload. If this don't discourage that pack — "

He squeezed down on a single trigger and heard the shot hailing against the boards — heard also, with grim satisfaction, the yell of warning and pain. The second barrel caught the troup a-scatter. Indigo swore delightedly and lifted the muzzle of his gun. But he held the fire until more Lingard men, attracted by the diversion, started to circle the barn. At that he let go. Shadows weaved and broke away. A return fusillade sang about the shed, wide and high. In the middle of the clearing one brazen voice was summoning his men.

"Black Clee," whispered Joe.

"We got 'em jumpin'."

"Come on."

They cleared the shed and slipped forward, barely catching sight of the Lingards streaming away from the barn. A hotter volley rose, smashing against the house harmlessly; and a clot of dirt struck Indigo fair in the face. So running, they poured buckshot across the meadow. Black Clee's summons rose more insistent and angry. A horse stampeded past the partners and then Joe struck Indigo a warning. "Back to the barricades. They're goin' to ride into us."

"Damned if I do! I'm too tired to run!"

The sullen quiver of the cavalcade rose against them. Joe let go with one barrel, veered the muzzle and squeezed down. Indigo, cooler than he would ever be in times of peace, let his fire lag just long enough to allow Joe opportunity for thumbing in fresh shells. The oncoming line grew raggedy, met the point-blank blast and of a sudden broke. Black Clee was cursing his heart away, the immense and frustrated temper raging against all men. Joe fired both barrels at once at the blank shadows and heard the rapid drumming fade away.

"Buckshot," he murmured, "is just plain mean."

"If I'm any judge, that's the last of that bunch tonight," opined Indigo. "They'll be lickin' their wounds from now till the saliva runs out. My Gawd, I'm shakin' like a pup. Let's get into the house."

"You go ahead. I want to catch this horse. Better scout the yard and see what you find."

Indigo rolled away, grumbling again. Joe turned up the meadow and located the stampeded horse at the barn door. He called through to the Marshalls inside. "All right, boys. The visit's over." Indigo gave a quick glance to the place. "Might find somethin'!"

Catching the horse, he spoke soothingly and stepped into the saddle, turning back for the main house porch. High above, the Lingard signal fire was dying for want of fuel, and as Joe watched it, rain sluicing against his set face, some grim, fatalistic thought kept running through his mind.

"The way of man. The fire of life runs high — for a little while. And then it's a long darkness."

He reined in at the porch and went inside to find the Marshall men grouping together and the women coming up. In a corner the three captives had been roped to chairs; and the woman with the bronze hair was ripping away the coat of the wounded one. She turned when Joe entered and without knowing why it was so, his glance went straight to her. A flash of some strange, remote emotion rose to the surface of her dark eyes and remained there a moment for him to see. Then it was gone, leaving Joe struggling with some old, old impulse that he thought had died in the first tempestuous, tragic flush of early youth. She turned back to the Lingard rider and Joe studied the competent play of her fingers, until Broderick Marshall's talk caught his attention.

"I don't see what we're a-goin' to do with these fellows. They're dead weight to us and they'll bring the Lingards back, sure as shootin'. Lingards look after Lingards. Make no mistake about it."

"They won't come again tonight," said Joe. "You can't whip up a bunch of men to that temper twice together."

"They'll bring us nothin' but grief," insisted Broderick Marshall. "More mouths to feed and not enough to eat as it is. And not enough ammunition to stave off another fight. Friend, this can't go on much longer."

"Not like this," agreed Joe quietly. "Give a set of men like the Lingards the whip and they'll use it. Take it away from them — and that's a different story. I intend to do that."

The attention of the room swung to him as he stood there, his thoughtful face deep in some speculation. Indigo looked at his partner sharply and sighed; he knew Joe and he knew what that gleam in Joe's eyes meant. And because he knew, he walked to the stove and put his back to it, soaking in the warmth. "Not afoot, Joe," he grumbled. "No sir, not afoot. I done all my walkin' for the next forty-five years."

"Break their idea of bein' upper dogs," mused Joe. "That's the thing. Hit and run and hit again."

"What with?" queried Broderick Marshall. "Got nothin' to hit with."

"You will have when my partner gets

through," opined Indigo, sourly. "That fellow wrote the book of rules. Don't *you* worry none. It's me that got the worryin' to do. I'm the buzzard he hauls into these scrapes."

"Better eat and sleep," said Marshall.

"Him?" scoffed Indigo. "Ha-ha! Watch me laugh."

One of the Marshall boys tramped through the broken door. "Found another horse in the clearin'. But if we pinked any of them they've been dragged off."

"Takes a lot of lead to hit anybody in a night scrape," observed Joe. "But I'll bet there's a ton of buckshot distributed in their hides. Bring that horse to the porch. We're usin' it now."

"I told you," groaned Indigo.

"Hit and run is the scheme," repeated Joe and raised his head. "And the best time to hit is right now. Come on, Indigo."

"Want more of us?" queried a younger Marshall, eager to renew the quarrel.

"Thanks, no. My partner and me have done this before and we're sort of established in the procedure." He looked to his gun and thumbed in fresh cartridges. "We'll be back in a little while. And how far is it to the mouth of the valley?"

"Mile and a half."

"We'll hail the house when we come back.

Better put out a couple of guards. One in the barn and one down the valley a little ways. Comin', Indigo?"

They went out together, stepped into the streaming wet saddles and turned southward through the rioting squall.

"And he's the man that talks peace in honeyed words," soliloquized Indigo to the vanished stars. "I said he was a hound for punishment some time back. But I wish to withdraw the remark, not meanin' to do any injustice to the hound. What's on your mind now?"

"Strike and run," said Joe. "Nothin' more serious than that. They won't be expecting us and they'll probably be holed up in that shanty, talkin' things over."

"So? I'd like to boost that shanty into the drink and float the whole cussed bunch out to sea. Tell you straight, Joe, my appetite for this sort of thing is plumb satisfied and they's so much water in me that I don't dare go near a fire for fear of warpin' clean out of shape."

They were immersed in the darkness and had no guide save the dim margin of the river directly to their left. Riding into small depressions, the water came stirrup high, and once they blindly forded a creek that hit along their legs. To either side the high barrier of the ridge pressed blacker and nearer.

"Indigo," mused the tall man in a muffled voice, "it ain't fair to ask a woman's age, but how old do you suppose that fine lady with the copper hair is?"

"Never seen her," stated Indigo, promptly. "*I* had my mind on business."

"Sometimes," went on Joe slowly, "a man rides many a dusty mile, never expectin' anything else. And then all of a sudden a fine, fair land opens up before him, and things are like he never expected to see again."

"Dusty!" snorted Indigo.

Joe had no answer. He was buried in his thoughts and though Indigo couldn't see across the interval, he felt his partner wrapped in the wistful reflections so characteristic of him. It disturbed Indigo, greatly. He was as jealous as a woman of their long association and instinctively bridled at any person or situation that threatened it.

Joe had mentioned a woman. Well, women played hell with men. There was no fighting them, no accounting for them. And Joe had only to smile to engage a woman's sympathy. Indigo had seen it often enough to know the magic of his partner's personality; more than once when he and Joe had ridden away from some place of rest, he had turned in the saddle to find a woman on a porch or a street, watching them go, standing quite still. Indigo knew why. Joe never turned to look but sometimes his silences lasted far out on the trail. As for the copper-haired lady, Indigo had lied glibly; he had seen her, and caught also his partner's unexpected interest. It worried him.

"Bluffs ahead," muttered Joe. "My bet is there's no body guardin' them right now. I'll go ahead."

The river swerved angrily into the narrowing throat; a dripping rock wall swept out to close away the meadow lands. Single file the partners took to the tricky footing and crawled on a good hundred yards before reaching the desert beyond. Abreast again, they walked the ponies on with a tightening of interest. The freshening wind, unchecked for long leagues, blasted against them and the driving pellets of rain struck with a needle-like force. And a yellow light winked through the pall.

"We better scout the shed and see how many horses are in it."

"You hold my horse and I'll amble on," decided Indigo. "I'm too damn skinny to sit still in this weather."

He disappeared. Joe saw his body pass across the lane of light once and after that the minutes dragged interminably. The shanty door opened and a man stepped out, going around the structure, at which Joe stiffened and swiftly considered his next move. But before he snapped into action the fellow came back with a load of wood, and presently sparks flew from the chimney. Then Indigo returned shaking himself like a terrier.

"Two horses. Two men. I took a peek in the back window."

"Rest of the outfit have hit the Cowcamp trail already, I reckon," observed Joe, drowsily. "Next question — is there anybody moochin' around this murk who's apt to stumble upon us durin' the next few minutes?"

"Want them buzzards in there?"

"That's on the ticket. Two less Lingards to scrap with. Two more horses. And some grub to truck back to the Marshalls, which is most important. Those women all looked hungry to me."

"Say, when the next chance comes I'm goin' to eat until my feet hurt."

Silently they pressed forward, drawing out of the shaft of light shimmering through the window. And, never bothering to stop and talk the business over, they closed within ten feet of the shanty, dismounted and walked to the very door. Joe's hand touched the latch softly and raised it a fraction of an inch by way of test. Indigo drew off somewhere, lost to Joe. But the big man knew his partner had taken a station by a window for emergency. So, lifting latch and gun at the same moment, he threw his weight forward, smashed through and confronted a pair of Lingards warming themselves at a red-bellied stove.

"Visit returned," drawled Joe; yet that phrase held a cutting edge and if the Lingards had failed to detect it they could never have missed the drilling quality of the eyes pressing so frigidly blue against them. They were at ease, slack-muscled and off-guard. And Joe's gun muzzle flipped upward slightly in command. Their arms lifted; he saw a sudden lust come into the face of one, a wild flash of recklessness that passed quickly or was throttled. The other was lumpishly indifferent.

"Nice boys," commended Joe. "Quick now — you, step forward. I don't like the smell of you. Step forward and turn!"

The rebellious one rose, advanced a pace and wheeled. Joe spoke again. "I know you want to argue this. I'm only reminding you it's open season around here and I've took out my shootin' license, big game and small. You're small game, brother, but you'll do.

234

Pulled painlessly."

The man yelled and lurched, but he had miscalculated the swiftness of Joe's arm as it leaped and retreated, holding a captured revolver. "You fool," grunted Joe. "Where's your head tonight? There's a gent outside itchin' to shoot your dumb head off. Back away. Cicero, you're next."

The other obeyed and was de-horned with equal dexterity. Indigo waddled through the door, water falling from his vast hat in a steady stream. He had brought a rope from one of the borrowed mounts and now methodically tied each Lingard, at elbow and wrist. The more obstreperous of the two winced at the hemp's bit and began to curse. Indigo cocked his head, listening with profound gravity.

"Not bad, brother. I can do that myself, but it's always a pleasure to listen in on new tunes. Your variety ain't much, but your expression is just dandy. Now come with me." He held them both at rope's end and pushed them out of the shanty. Joe swept the place with a practiced eye. Fresh mud all over the place — and a trace of blood on one bunk. Ripping a blanket off the nearest, he laid it on the floor and swept into it a side of bacon, several cans of food, a sack of sugar, and every odd article and package on the table or in the cupboard. He pouched it all and slung the blanket over his shoulder; Indigo was waiting outside.

"Tied them boys to their own horses. I got a jerk line on 'em. How about burnin' this dump?"

"No-o, better not. Might make them just mad enough to try again. We got a night's sleep comin'."

"Oh, you do sleep, do you?"

They pressed forward, re-entered the valley and traversed the slushy footing rapidly. Joe hailed from a distance and steered a course by a guarded reply. The house door opened on them and they went in, leaving the horses to the sentry.

"Me," declared Indigo, "I'd like a cup of coffee. How about it, Joe?"

"Think I'd rather sleep," murmured Joe. The copper-haired woman stood up from a chair and lifted one white hand. Joe followed up the stairs to where she threw open a door. When he turned, he saw the outline of her body against the light reflected from below. Nothing more than that. But the last pressure of her fingers was on his shoulder and the slow, lazy tones of her voice dissolved the chill of his bones.

"Sleep well — Joe. And goodnight."

Chapter Five

Another gray afternoon swirled and beat against the beleaguered Marshall house. That day a dozen scattered rifle bullets came singing out of the ridge rim and futilely struck the barn, the dwelling and the random out-structures. Yet so accustomed were the people of this forlorn valley to such insolence that they neither flinched nor were interested. Joe, warming his wet feet by the kitchen stove, debated this indifference with himself and came to a conclusion.

"Trouble is, you boys are takin' too much for granted. Death and taxes, folks say, are plumb sure to come. But why add the Lingards to that list? Ain't a one of you which doesn't expect to cave in sooner or later to 'em. Unhealthy state of mind. When a man starts thinkin' he's done — then he's in a bad way."

The whole clan — save for three stationed

at the barn — were in the kitchen. Now and then some of the menfolk had gone crouching outside and back again. Yet it was a pitifully inadequate show of activity and thirty-seven days of such scurrying had left its mark upon them. Nearly all showed a sullenly beaten look. Black Clee had crushed them with a strange weapon and, from his post on the ridge or his cabin at the valley's mouth, waited for the inevitable disintegration and surrender. Joe knew they could fight; he had seen that proved. It was the insistent pressure that ruined their fibers, and the despairing knowledge that their womenfolk were caught in the same trap. And that was the second of his audible observations.

"Was it just you boys alone, you'd cut and run. Blaze a hole through those scoundrels. But you can't move for fear of what will happen to the women."

"Your intellect shines like a fallin' star," grumbled Indigo, as touchy as a spooked horse. A day of this dull waiting was nearly more than his nature could stand.

"One of those double-barreled compliments," drawled Joe. "I'm bright but I don't last long, is that it? A nasty one, Indigo."

"I was a-thinkin' of all them tons o' wood we ricked around our cabin."

Broderick Marshall rocked himself in a corner chair, chin fallen forward, scarcely a trace of animation in his body. The fighting sap was out of him. Being old he had no recuperative powers; he could not fight, rest and wake refreshed to fight again. The elastic in him had been stretched too far and held taut too long. Some particular word of Joe's lazy talk broke into the dead center of his despairing mind and woke him.

"Thirty-seven days like this. And fifteen years back of that. Every hour — figgerin' what the Lingards was a-goin' to do next. Enough to make a man queer, specially when he sees his kinfolk and his sons go down one by one. That bunch, every one of 'em is born killers. We held 'em off last night, we beat 'em back. But what good is it? There they are today, still hangin' on. We never could beat the Lingards. We can't now."

"Easy," cautioned Joe, hearing the near break in the old man's voice. And he squinted thoughtfully around the room. "Ten and two is twelve. Indigo and me makes fourteen. You can do a lot of damage with that many."

"What good's fourteen men? We can't muster six rounds of ammunition to the man. This mornin' before daylight we butchered our last pindlin', runty beef. When that's gone we're through. These children ain't had a drop of milk for five weeks. That's what hurts the most! I could cut the livin' heart of a Lingard!"

"Now you begin to show some spirit," applauded Joe.

"We're licked," said the old man, sinking back apathetically.

Joe seemed wholly relaxed, yet his mind was worrying around the problem like a terrier attacking a ball. "You've been jammed against this problem for so long you can't back away far enough to see the landscape in general. Your idea is to stay and take it. Mine ain't."

"You just mention another idea," suggested one of the younger Marshalls gloomily.

"What I'm tryin' to figure is Lingard's next move," drawled Joe. "Half the battle is beatin' a man to his own play. What would you do, Indigo, if you was Lingard?"

"Attack again," was Indigo's prompt answer.

"Yeah. That's your style. But it ain't Black Clee's. He's another type of animal. He's an Indian for figurin'. Nobody but an Indian-minded fellow would think up this siege business and hold at it for so long."

"Well, what would you do, if you was him?" demanded Indigo.

"Continue the siege," responded Joe, equally prompt. "He's got everything to gain and nothin' to lose. What puzzles me is why he attacked last night and broke up his original plan."

Indigo had an answer for that. "Because you and me made him awful mad. He figgered we'd got down here and that set off the fireworks."

"Correct. Now, is he still mad enough to make another attack, or is he just mad enough to stand up yonder and wait?"

"Oh, my Gawd, don't ask me no more questions," grunted Indigo. "I'm about — "

Three evenly spaced shots echoed near the house. Indigo sprang for the basement door and Joe rose quietly. But Broderick Marshall only shook his head. "That's their signal. Wait and see."

Silence fell over the place for a long five minutes. Then the outer basement door squealed and a Marshall guard came slowly up the stairs. "Same thing," he muttered.

"What's that?" Joe asked.

"They send a man down the slope every once in a while to dicker," said the guard. "Same story this time with one exception. They'll quit the fight and let us live peaceable if we agree to the original article."

"Go back and tell them we're not barterin' our womenfolks!" shouted a younger Marshall. "No, by God, not till the last shot's fired!"

"My daughter," added Broderick Marshall with a sullenly defeated air, "ain't for sale."

Joe looked across the room. The woman with the copper-colored hair stood with her back to the wall, erect and with slow color coming to her cheeks. But there was a sudden fear in her fine eyes — the first time Joe had observed it. Unaccountably the harsh fires of his sleeping temper began to burn hot. So this was Black Clee's article of surrender. The lines about his face tightened. Man and woman looked at each other across the distance, steadily, something passing between those two calm people.

"Great guns, what kind of a bunch are them Lingards?" demanded Indigo, absolutely staggered.

"Killers," said Broderick Marshall and fell silent.

"They're overplayin' their hand," said Joe very softly and let out a great breath. The shadows were deepening and it was lamplight time. The copper-haired woman moved with soft grace to touch a match to a waiting wick; the tall partner's attention followed her, even while hearing a Marshall mutter: "Wonder how my house is by now?"

Joe's whip-like question startled them all. "What house?"

"Mine," said the man. "Two miles up,

beyond the rapids, at the end of the valley."

"As easy to protect as this one?" challenged Joe.

"About."

Joe's long body straightened above them all. A small current of excitement passed through the room. "Then," said he, "there's our answer. Lingard expects us to stay here and get beaten. You expect to stay here and get beaten. You can't make a play on account of the women. But if you had a place to hide your women, you could sally out and smash into the Lingards. When dark comes this ranch moves out. Up to that house. We will leave two or three boys in charge. The rest of us hit back to make a play."

"They'll discover we made a shift," said a younger Marshall.

"It's our part to see they don't," replied Joe. "We do this under dark. They won't find anything until tomorrow mornin' at least. And by then it'll be too late for them."

"Once we leave this house we're lost," muttered the old man.

"Stay here another night and you're lost," countered Joe. "And Black Clee is just bankin' on you doin' that exact stunt."

"Dark's about come," said Indigo, rousing up from his moroseness at the proposal of activity.

"They got men posted between us and that house," said Broderick Marshall. "At the rapids where the trail narrows down."

"My partner and I will take care of those fellows," was Joe's brittle reply. "Now, get a good husky fire in this stove that will shoot sparks for half the night. Catch up the things you'll need for a couple of days. Send some boys out to saddle the horses. In a half hour we'll be on our way."

"Can't be done," said the old man. "Too dangerous. No tellin' what we'll run into."

Joe's jaw hardened. He thought he had failed to stir them; he thought then they were beyond the power to take the only fighting chance left. Some of the younger men stirred anxiously, but Broderick Marshall was shaking his head, asserting all there was left of his authority. And at that disheartening moment the cool, sure voice of the copper-haired woman broke the lethargic spell.

"It will be done."

"Marie — "

"Yes. I have something to say, haven't I? I've waited all this time for some single way out. To stay here is to starve and give in. For me, it is worse than that. You are all tired and without hope. Let these two men plan for us. They know. Get up, Dad. Nothing can be worse than now. Not even to be killed on the way."

Broderick Marshall stared at his daughter for several moments. A sudden gleam came to his eyes. "Let it be so. Seems to be one fighter left in the family."

"This is goin' to be damn ticklish business," whispered Indigo, standing beside Joe in the basement. "I sure wouldn't like those fellas to know how plumb uncertain I feel about it. Lots of things which has got to work just right or we're blown higher'n a kite."

"Chances to take," agreed Joe, working the breech of a rifle.

"There's them five prisoners of ours which we can't leave behind and which might start bellerin' at the wrong minute if we take 'em. There's those fellas at the rapids to choke off. There's that house itself, which may be lousy with Lingards when we get there. There's also the chance some of that black bunch may be skulkin' around here this minute watchin' us."

"The first prisoner to talk out loud gets a cracked skull. You and I have got to get whatever guards may be at the rapids. No ifs or ands. We've got to get 'em. As to the house when we reach it — that's our gamble. But I don't figure anybody's in it.

Else why should they watch the trail at the rapids so close?"

"And what're we a-goin' to do when we get there?" insisted Indigo.

"Our bright and sunny friend."

"I'm just thinkin' ahead," protested Indigo. "Well, it's plumb dark enough to line the belly of a cat."

The outer basement door opened to admit a slim, anxious Marshall. "Horses is ready. We better clatter along before the old man changes his mind."

"Set," agreed Joe. "Go up and herd your folks out here. My partner and me will walk ahead."

They went through the door and softly along the barricade to the barn. Joe's roving glance struck constantly out to the left where the foot of the bluff lay unseen in the black mist and rain haze. Wind whipped down from the north and he could hear the river slicing its turbulent way along its flooded banks. At the barn's back door they were softly challenged by the remaining Marshall on guard.

"How's it go?" queried Joe.

"Their signal fire ain't burnin'," muttered the guard. "Looks queer to me."

Horses moved uneasily inside. Indigo muttered ominously and groped about for reins.

The Marshalls were filing in and a child cried in a kind of choked fear; Joe's lips compressed his instant sympathy feeding the enormously growing fire of his temper. Men were made to take the shock and the punishment of living, but to see a woman's eyes cloaked by dread and to hear a youngster crying — these were things that upset every monitor of caution in his level brain. At the moment he closed the door on all scruples and his lifelong instinct of fairness. The Lingards were killers, an avenging breed without conscience or pity. They were outlawed from every consideration of decency. They had the justice of killers coming to them. Nothing else.

"You hear me, Indigo? Everything goes from now on. They ain't givin' quarter and they'll get none."

"I'm just one jump ahead of you," grunted the little man. "Decided that some time back. Well?"

Joe lifted his voice slightly. "Get those five prisoners?"

"Yeah."

"Double 'em up on the horses and tie 'em to stay. One of you boys ride beside each pair. They go to the front of your party and if there's any firin' done they'll take the bullets first. And if there's so much

247

as a sound from any one, smash in their heads. I mean that — all five, and waste no time about it. Now get organized. Ride close together. My partner and me goes ahead. One of you fellows follow in exactly five minutes as a connecting link. In ten minutes the rest of you come along. If you hear one or two shots, never mind, just plug right along. If the shootin' gets general turn back and forget all about us. Set a walkin' gait and keep it. And don't lose your nerve. We're on our way."

The partners sallied out the front door into the driving tempest, turned north and were lost in a pit of darkness. The river, swollen with its cargo from every jutting creek along the ridges, had backed farther into the meadow and their ponies walked fetlock deep all the way. Some undermined section of the sandy earth gave way with a sharp, sundering sound and was torn into the racing stream. Indigo muttered dourly.

"Trouble in this damn affair for you and me, Joe. I feel it. If them Marshalls fall into a trap and they's some shootin' I ain't goin' to stop till I've planted a flock of them black buzzards under the sod."

"Double," said Joe.

"Well," insisted Indigo, "it might happen. That Black Clee ain't a fool. And where in thunder are we goin' to locate them guards at the rapids? Like huntin' for a drop o' water in the ocean."

"The other day when we passed along the rim of the ridge," replied Joe, "I saw a brush hut right where the trail hits the side of the rapids. They'll be in it, if any place. But we've got to get 'em quiet if we can."

"Then what — " began Indigo. But he was stopped by Joe's pressing arm. In silence they rose with the trail and left the overflowed meadow behind. The river dropped down a bank and the smash of the rapids grew louder. To the ridge side they saw trees pressing dimly in. And upthrust boulders began to march beside them until the pressure forced them single file, Joe leading. Then this narrow ledge let out into the wider ground and the partners were halted, guns out, before some blurred and mysterious obstruction. Joe dismounted and threw his reins to Indigo, whispering, "Stick fast a minute."

Crouching on, step at a time, he arrived in front of the brush hut. From his previous view of it he knew it was nothing more than a lean-to covered with pine boughs and closed in on three sides. The fourth side, open and unprotected, now yawned at him; and as he poised within ten yards of the place his nostrils picked up the dim trace of woodsmoke. But there was no gleam of coals and no movement of figures, nor any sounds of guards. Stepping aside, he came closer, eyes straining to penetrate the tricky pall; and at last he stood against a corner pole with head and gun hooked around the corner. There was nothing in the hut but a round object; going in he found it to be a galvanized wash tub upended and slightly warm. Obviously it was to cloak a fire, for vent holes had been punched in the top and the sides.

He circled the hut, covered the intervening ground to the river and poked back to the parapet of rocks on the ridge side. Then, following these rocks, he advanced a hundred yards, tested two or three short alleys leading into them, and came back to rake the level ground with several quick diagonal trips that carried him to the hut once more. Horse and rider loomed atop him; a deep, gruff voice muttered. *"Quien es?"* Joe sprang back, and then swore.

"Fooled me. Nobody right here, Indigo. You wait for the Marshall lad to come along. Then cruise on straight ahead. I'm goin' to push yonder afoot."

Indigo grunted a warning. "I dislike this gettin' disconnected a heap."

But Joe was gone, forging ahead in long

strides. Beyond the area already scouted he began to veer and inspect the land in a staggering, stair-stepped course that brought him to the river's edge and then to the foot of the bluff. He looked for trails leading up the ridge and found none; he tested rock bays for ambush; and all the while there was an uneasy feeling of insecurity in his head. Guards had been in that hut not long before. What reason had caused them to withdraw and where were they now? Putting himself in Black Clee Lingard's shoes he could see no alternatives other than to continue the siege or to make a second attack. Yet when he considered the man he could not help feeling the chance of some surprise.

"I'd know better if I had an idea what this country looked like," he told himself. "Dangerous business all around, but nothin' else to do."

The meadow widened, the trees and rocks began to draw back. Conscious that he had no great amount of time to waste he abandoned that half of the meadow on the river side and concentrated his attention along the trees. There was still no trail and no likely place where the Lingards might be waiting. So, for the course of some hundred yards he stalked; and then in the foreground he saw a flash of light. The upper Marshall house stood just ahead.

Occupied by Lingards. That upset the whole course of his plan, and for a moment he stood absolutely still, debating. But though he sought swiftly along the possibilities open to him, he could find nothing new. Either go ahead or turn back. Watching the light closely and using it for a guide he slid diagonally over the meadow until he stood by a porch corner of the place. The shaft of light, he discovered, came from a back kitchen window and he crawled beside the wall until his eyes were level with a crack in a drawn shade. Inside were three men of Black Clee's killer outfit, one playing solitaire, another sitting idle and the third about to lift a pot of coffee from a red stove.

His first reaction was one of grim satisfaction, for if there were no more Lingards about, this trio could be bagged without any undue commotion. Probably they had withdrawn from the hut by the rapids to get warm, slacking off their vigilance and disobeying Black Clee's instructions. Considering the misery of remaining abroad in a night like this, such negligence was both human and understandable. And Joe, seeing the glow of the stove fire and the coffee steaming in cups, was the more acutely aware of his own discomfort.

Yet there was still scouting to do and no time to lose. In a very little while the Marshalls would be piling up on him. Therefore, he ducked beneath the window, kept on until he had reached the back of the building and discovered the open door of a woodshed ten feet away. Horses in there; he heard them. Going over, he put his head through and listened. Their uneasy shifting came through the black and the champing of their teeth on the bits. Though he could not see at all he knew that three animals would make a tight fit for the shed.

There still remained the possibility of more men in the house and more horses in the barn. Quickly cutting across the back of the house he oriented himself by a tall and peaked shadow ahead. The door of this too stood open but he could detect no kind of movement inside. And with that information he swung back to intercept Indigo's approach.

Fifty yards down the meadow moving figures, many of them, almost overran him. Indigo's quick, *"Quien es?"* shot out.

"What the devil have you brought along?" demanded Joe.

"The whole gang caught up with me," grunted Indigo. "All of a sudden they're rarin' to fight."

"We can't keep the women and kids in

this weather all night," broke in one of the Marshalls. "By God, if we got to blast a way through this valley, all right! But we got to git shelter."

"Three of that bunch in the house," said Joe. "Indigo, you come with me. Rest of you hit into the barn for a minute. The big door's open."

Indigo slid to the ground and marched forward. The two came to the kitchen window, Joe looked in to verify the scene and then, tapping Indigo briefly on the shoulder, drew quietly away. The little partner adapted himself instantly to the situation and took his station by the window with the muzzle of his gun bearing upon the pane and his body drawn as far out of the passing beam of light as possible. Time dragged interminably and he wondered what took Joe so long; meanwhile the Lingard men were seated at the table and drinking coffee with a relish that made Indigo's mouth water. One of the trio laughed, whereat Indigo's dislike increased mightily and he swore to himself silently.

By stretching his neck a little it was just possible to see the door through which Joe would come in, and as the moments wore on the grip on his gun tightened until the pressure ran from wrist to shoulder. The laughing man suddenly sobered and turned his head, half rising. Indigo took a full bead on him as the door flashed open and Joe's tall, reassuring form stepped into the yellow light of the room. The two still in their chairs never ventured to move, but the third's elbow crooked with a savage speed; and Indigo's bullet crashed through the pane and caught that renegade cold in the shoulder, sending him spinning back upon the stove. There was no more resistance, and Indigo raced around for the door.

The Marshalls were streaming over from the barn as he sprang into the room and like a terrier broke past Joe to disarm the three. Joe's quiet drawl released the tension.

"Sorry for that shot. Don't want to attract any attention on this house tonight. You fellows have done your last fightin'. Any more of you around these parts?"

"Find that out for yourself," snapped the punctured one. He wheeled savagely on Indigo. "You played hell with my arm!"

"You don't know good luck when it hits you," snorted Indigo and dexterously unbuckled the fellow's belt. "Might have been your neck. What next, Joe? We're collectin' a lot o' specimens but we ain't struck pay ore yet."

Joe watched the trio closely. One of them, now backed in a corner, shifted his head slightly and seemed to be listening for sounds out in the storm. Meeting Joe's glance, he lowered his head and assumed a sullen indifference. But the tall partner's eyes gleamed with swift interest, and he rapped out an order to the first Marshall coming in. "Get your women here."

"What next?" repeated Indigo.

"We've got eight of these buzzards now. That's eight less to buck. Lingard's gang can't grow on bushes. Marshall, how many men can he muster in a pinch?"

"Mebbe thirty, drawin' in everybody from the odd spots of the country."

"Subtract eight," reflected Joe. "Subtract five more I'm plain sure we put temporarily out of commission last night and they dragged off. Leaves around seventeen men. We're gettin' down to a fifty-fifty basis. Here's three more belts of cartridges to distribute. Then — "

The women came filing in. Joe disappeared through another door to inspect the house and tramped back, preoccupied. "Better divide those cartridges among you." And he ducked out the back, Indigo following.

"What the hell's on your mind, Joe?"

"We're goin' to leave two boys here and ride with the rest. Tonight's our night to do some smashing. There may be another

Lingard or so moochin' around the woods
— in fact, I think there is, judgin' from the
look I caught from one of those buzzards.
But I'm laying stakes on the fact that Black
Clee's main bunch is in Cowcamp on a war
parley right now. Otherwise why wouldn't
the fire be burnin' on the ridge? Well, if
he's in Cowcamp, he can't have such a great
lot of force, for he's had to leave somebody
stoppin' the gap at the lower end of the
valley and maybe a man or so at the top.
So we strike Cowcamp! You go back and
tell the Marshalls that — but don't let the
Lingards hear you. Get 'em all organized to
ride. I'll be back in a minute. Want to scout
the meadow once more."

He disappeared around the shed suddenly.
Indigo walked to the threshold of the kitchen
door and solemnly called the nearest Marshalls outside, grunting his orders at them.
"And don't argue the point with me, I'm
just a-tellin' you what my partner says. When
he figures it's high time to smack into trouble
you better believe it's right."

"Yeah, but just two men to stick with the
womenfolk?"

"Can't take a town with three men and
a small boy," opined Indigo. "You better
play Joe's cards."

"Well — "

One shot rolled suddenly back upon them, coming out of the damp ridge side. Indigo started as if he had been struck and raced around the shed. "Joe — hey, Joe!"

But there was no answer.

Chapter Six

Stepping around the shed and through the drive of this miserable, comfortless night, Joe walked into the narrowing mouth of a trail that climbed steeply up. This, he knew, was the upper outlet from the valley, which he had been seeking during the last few hours; the way to the ridge's backbone. It was not his intention to pursue it far. He only wanted to reassure himself of its immediate safety and to determine if he could whether or not there were other members of the Lingard outfit skulking about.

He advanced along the steep grade a matter of yards, touched now and then by sweeping pine boughs that spilled their load of water upon him. The clash of the wind, the steady wash of rain and the ripping boom of the river drowned out every lesser sound; beyond arm's length nothing was to be seen. In this situation his normal senses helped him little and he fell back upon that uncanny, animal-like perception sharpened through years of usage and experience. He sidled away from obstructions by the very feel of them advancing against him. And now and then he stopped to square himself with the trail. Looking back he caught and lost a single beam of light from the house.

It was only a moment's pause, but it brought disaster upon him. Even as he swung to go forward he felt an invisible body moving against him; and before he could move aside, before he could so much as raise his gun he collided full with another walker in the night. The man was moving rapidly and the impact sent a checked breath and grunt out of him. Joe wrenched back, too late to miss the other's swiftly imprisoning arms. A cry of surprise and warning beat into the night.

"Link — come 'ere — I got one of the yella-bellied — Hold still you, or I'll rip open your guts! Link — hey Link!"

Joe braced his feet and threw himself and the grasping man down the grade. They struck the slushy earth, careened into the drenched bushes and fought savagely, arm wrenching against arm. The man's cry beat up again for the help of an obscure partner; his knees tore into Joe's flanks and one fist raked across Joe's face. It was brute fighting;

rolling and tearing and clawing on down the trail with first the tall partner on top and then the Lingard, whose stubborn grip would not be discouraged. A shot broke through the sluggish darkness and boots sloshed nearer.

"You hammer-headed fool, stop that shootin'!" panted the first Lingard, forcing all of his weight into Joe's throat. "Come here — stick a gun in his ribs! No — not me — git down here and poke him!"

"Got you," muttered the other Lingard partisan, voice trembling with excitement. "Hold still or I'll make bird bait outa you!"

The gun bit into Joe's chest and he felt the quiver of the hand that held it; this fellow seemed to have a bad case of buck fever and Joe stopped struggling instantly, knowing the danger of further resistance. One of them ripped away his gun and un-buckled his belt. Down the trail Indigo's high yell came beating.

"Joe — hey, Joe!"

Pressure was removed from his prone body. A quick throaty order struck him. "Git up! Move over into the bushes! Keep your mouth shut, understand? Keep that gun against him, Link! Git off the trail — hold it now — !"

Indigo's hail sounded nearer. Joe, jammed into the brush and held vice-like between his two captors, heard the slush of his partner's feet coming along. Directly abreast, Indigo sounded again. The Lingards were in frozen postures as the little man went by, near enough to be touched, yet invisible. A breathless murmur passed between the Lingards "Get him, too?"

"Stand fast. May be others around. Shut up — "

Indigo came back on the run and was swallowed by the distance. At that, the Lingards moved in unison, shoved Joe to the trail and pushed him along. "Trot up, brother. No monkeyshines and no delay. Run faster. We ain't goin' to fall into the hands of your gang. Faster!"

One was ahead, slipping and sliding and breathing hard — the same excitable fellow with the buck fever. "Young at this game," Joe thought to himself and calculated his chances of diving off the trail; but the second Lingard's gun kept painfully jabbing him from behind and the second Lingard's intermittent spurts of warning discouraged the idea. The trail steepened, but the pace kept increasing until Joe's legs ached and his lungs sucked vainly for extra air. Plainly his captors feared ambush and pursuit as they clawed at the flank of the ridge. But Joe heard no sound from behind to assure him that Indigo was on the road. He knew his partner's method of thinking very well; Indigo would lose no time, but before striking up the trail the little man would first do some preliminary scouting around the house to avoid going on a wild goose chase. As fiery and tempestuous as Indigo was, he nevertheless had a cool head in a crisis. It would take —

His reasoning was interrupted by the sudden leveling of the trail. They had arrived at the summit, all three badly winded. A challenge came from ahead, soft and sudden. The Lingard behind him answered and Joe saw two other dim figures come into vague view.

"We caught one of 'em on the trail," said the more energetic of the two captors. "Ran smack into him while we was goin' down to find out what the shootin' meant. Know what's happened? The Marshalls have shifted to the upper house, that's what!"

"The hell! What about the boys at the lean-to then?"

"Guess they're took into camp."

"That ain't right," reflected one of the others. "The shootin' come from the house, not from the lean-to. What would our fellas be doin' off their stampin' ground?"

"Probably ducked back to keep warm."

"Wait till Black Clee hears about that,"

was the ominous rejoinder. "Well, who've you got here? Which one o' the rats is it?"

"Dunno. What's your name, fella?"

"Wouldn't know it if I told you," said Joe.

"One o' them strangers!" exclaimed a Lingard. "And wait till Black Clee hears about *that!* So the Marshalls have shifted? What good will it do 'em? From the fryin' pan to the fire. We better shake into Cowcamp and notify Clee."

"Somebody's got to stick here and watch," protested the energetic Lingard.

"What for? They ain't goin' to go no place. How far can they ride on starved horses? Be good if they did hit out. We'd have 'em hipped in the open by daylight. That's what Clee's been hopin' for this long month."

"Well, we better move afore they bust right into us. Somebody get the ponies."

A figure made off and presently reappeared with the animals trailing behind. They mounted one at a time. "Put a rope around him and cinch it tight. I'll take him in front of me."

"A wise guy," muttered another. "But I never saw these wise guys wiggle clear of Clee any quicker'n the rest. You sure will pay by the neck for that amusement in the saloon, mister. Tall trees and a quick drop.

We'll just separate that massive intellect from its moorin's. Step up."

Joe, painfully pinched around the arms and waist, was half thrown up in front of a rider who took the further precaution of snubbing the rope's end around the horn. Then the group veered, sidled left and right and went single file into a tunnel-like trace. Nobody spoke. The ground descended considerably and after a while they left the trees to the rear and set across the prairie at a racking pace; the storm slatted gustily against them. The tall partner let himself go slack while his mind plucked at the possibilities. He had no illusions as to what the Lingards would do with him. It was only a question of time; and time suddenly became the single precious thread that held him to life. Indigo would be on the trail, no doubt of that. But there would be delay and groping and false leads and perplexed questioning. In the ridge were a hundred trails, any one of which might draw the small partner's attention.

"How will he know the Lingards have all gone to Cowcamp?" Joe asked himself. "He ain't got a blessed hint to work from. Be plumb natural for him to figure I'm salted away up in the trees with the rest of the pack. Nothin' to tell him this bunch has shifted tactics." There was nothing to guide

Indigo — nothing except a power of direct-ness in the little man that sometimes drove him straight ahead. There was hope in that. Indigo hated to sit down and reason things out; he was too impatient, too prone to get on his horse and start off in a direct line. And if tonight Indigo obeyed that instinct, he would race for Cowcamp to blast it apart. "Damn small hope in that," Joe reflected. "He might spend the rest of the night scourin' the ridge instead."

Once, after an immeasurably tedious stretch of time, the group was nearly rammed by a rider outbound from town, who was in their midst before checking his gait. A moment's soft-voiced parley took place and then the newcomer turned and joined them on the inbound trip. Talk rose and fell fitfully behind Joe but the wind obscured the meaning of it and he was gripped in a half frozen lethargy that relaxed his vigilance. The speed increased and over the plain the wink of a light showed, at which the Lingards seemed to take fresh life and energy. They swung a trifle to correct the course, hit the street and drew up in front of the saloon, stiffly dismounting. Somebody walked across the street while they were unfastening Joe and by a beam of light he made out the stable tender's leering, sullen cheeks fixed on him with malign pleasure.

"Didn't expect to see us again, after cuttin' your didoes, eh? You'll learn — you'll learn."

"March through," grunted another, and Joe shouldered the saloon doors aside and stepped into the grateful warmth of the place. He had the thought at the moment that his eyes were playing tricks with him. This scene had not changed by so much as a hair from the one twenty-four hours back. The same men sat at the tables in the same lackadaisical postures, the same Mexican lay sprawled on the floor by the stove. The gambler looked inscrutably over the room, fingering his chips; and Black Clee Lingard faced him from the bar, dark eyes a-flicker with temper.

"I told you I never let a man go," he stated evenly. For a moment his pride would not let him give way, then all the vindictive, outraged authority in him blazed out and flamed through the silent room. "I gave you fair warnin' not to meddle! I said it plain as words could be — and you got the idee back there in the shanty. Never say I didn't give you a fair chance! Since it wasn't your style to let me and mine alone, now take the consequences!"

"What might that be?" drawled Joe.

Black Clee's face tightened and all the savage will of the man expressed itself in the flare of his nostrils — like some animal keening the blood-tainted wind or setting himself for the spring of death. "Want to know that, do you? It will be a ride out on the prairie with a couple of my men beside you. Just a mile ride and a bullet between the shoulders!"

"Proud of yourself," mused Joe, studying Black Clee's suddenly wolfish eyes. "Never been bucked very hard before, have you? Never been crossed."

"Some have tried it," snapped Black Clee, white teeth clicking together.

"And mebbe have taken that mile ride out on the prairie," suggested Joe. He was very grave, the lean cheeks cut with deep, diagonal lines. The blue eyes bored into Black Clee, hard and probing, as if he sought to fathom what predatory, sinister impulses passed through the man's brain.

Black Clee's doubled fist struck the top of the bar mightily; the dozing Mexican started up from the floor and drew into a darker corner step by step while the watchful gambler's fingers froze around the clacking chips. Black Clee stepped forward, rage creating a repulsive battleground on his face.

"Stand there!" he shouted. "Stand there and figger to stare me down! By God, I have ripped the heart out of better men than you! You may be a hard gent where you come from, but in *my* territory you're nothin' but a yella dog! I run this country — my word turns the wheel! I have run this end of the country for twenty-five years and they ain't a soul big enough to stop me now. I make men and I break 'em. The Marshalls are findin' that out. When I'm through they won't be nothin' but a memory around here! And the buzzards will be pickin' your bones tomorrow!"

The great paw swept up from the bar, palm wide open, and struck Joe on the side of the face. The echo of it shot through the room like a gun report; the tall partner rocked on his heels and caught himself from falling. And then the dead silence seemed to deepen. Black Clee had thrust his jaw forward and glared at Joe intently, waiting for a reply, waiting for a move.

Joe shook his head, feeling the needles of pain jab into his flesh. A film cleared from his eyes, and he was droning a soft reply. "Even a man with a good hand sometimes overplays it. But no man with any sense ever overplays it twice runnin' — which you have done, my friend."

"Talk," he grunted. And then the terrific temper subsided before a thin, sardonic grin.

"Think of the barkeep your friend killed — think of him when you fall out of the saddle tonight." He swung on the nearest partisan and spat an order. "Go get Flash out of bed. This is his job. You'll ride with him, Willy."

One of Joe's captors, long silent, ventured to break in. "What I wanted to tell you, Clee, was the Marshalls have deserted the main house. They're up at the high end, in Bird Marshall's place."

"Why in hell didn't you speak before?" shouted Black Clee, raging again. His glance raked the whole party. "What you all doin' here? Who's guardin' that ridge? Great Judas, have I got to whip — "

"Wasn't no chance to get a word in till now," replied the other sullenly. "We boys all come in because there wasn't no use in stayin'. You wanted 'em to break out of the meadow, didn't you? Well, it looks like they might try such a stunt. We'll have 'em hipped. They can't get far with old horses and a pack of women."

"Bright boy," was Black Clee's sarcastic retort. "Since when did *you* take to thinkin'?"

"Well — "

"Shut up. I'll supply the brains for this outfit. Wonder you didn't sleep through the night afore tellin' me. So they moved." He swung on Joe. "Some of your ideas, I reckon. Had a bright thought about sneakin' around us, eh? They'll thank you a heap when I run 'em to earth. And what've you done with my men?"

"Teachin' 'em manners," replied Joe softly. "Which is a lesson you need likewise. And might get yet."

Black Clee glowered. "I have got a notion to take a strip o' hide off your back for every one of them boys. Too damn bad torture ain't in style these days, or I would. Now you had some slick ideas in your bonnet when you moved them Marshalls. What was it? Spit it out!"

"You said you was supplyin' the brains for the outfit," returned Joe casually. "So put that massive intellect to work and find out."

"Another remark like that and I'll break your skull like an egg," threatened Black Clee, face dark as thunder.

Joe held his peace. Black Clee stood rooted, hostile eyes stabbing against the tall man; alternate expressions of craftiness and anger played over his face. Presently he turned to the room. "Roust out. Get some grub in your bellies and saddle up. Wake the rest of the boys."

The crowd rose and went reluctantly away from the warmth; there was some confusion at the door and a pair of men elbowed in — one being the messenger just dispatched and the other a heavy-lidded giant with the face of a stubborn horse. Black Clee permitted himself another knife-like grin. "Here's business for you, Flash. Get your horse and take this fine gentleman for a little pleasure trip. He wants to see our country. Willy's goin' along with you."

The giant Flash seemed too slow witted to speak on the spur of the moment. He rounded the bar and poured himself a drink, all the while measuring Joe with a nerveless glance. Joe's muscles constricted at the inspection. He had seen his share of killers, he had measured wits with them and tested their impulses. But this stolid creature behind the bar scarcely displayed a ray of human intelligence; he was cold, apparently without conscience, without more than a rudimentary thinking apparatus. And there he stood, surveying his victim with the dull gaze of a butcher measuring a bullock about to be slaughtered. A machine of destruction that killed on order just as he would have lifted an arm on order. Black Clee's cold amusement deepened.

"There's the end o' your caperin', friend.

When I say a thing I mean it."

"So?" mused Joe. "Your chore boy seems able to work alone. Why send this Willy along?"

"To bring Flash in from the rain afterwards," said Clee contemptuously. "He don't think of more'n one thing at a time. His arms work but his head don't." He spoke more slowly to the giant. "Go get your horse, Flash."

Flash lumbered out, shouldering through the doors as if they never existed. Willy stood still and watched Joe, cat-like. Black Clee went around the bar, restored to self-satisfaction, and poured a pair of glasses, one of which he shoved across to Joe.

"Here's to all wise fellas like you," he rumbled. "But I never saw the wise gent nor the hard gent that didn't find his match soon enough."

"That might be your little swan song," remarked Joe and downed the drink. Black Clee stared over the space, suspicion flickering in again. But he had nothing more to say then. Joe walked to the stove and placed his back to it, grateful for the warmth. Men came back one at a time, shaking the water from them. Outside he heard the rumble of talk and an occasional curse. Overhead the wind wrenched at the rickety roof and rain drummed steadily against wall and window.

The gambler had turned to look, white fingers splayed idly on the table. Buried as he was in his speculations, Joe thought he saw some signal of sympathy or understanding in the man's ivory cheeks, but to that he paid little attention. He was trying to picture the actions of Indigo. He was certain of one thing — Indigo was at the present moment lifting heaven and earth to find him. The little partner was too quick on the trigger, too belligerent a fighter to let any grass grow under his feet. But the night held a thousand snares and the darkness might beckon a hundred different ways. Help from that direction was too problematical to even nourish with hope; as for help of any other kind, there was none. Cowcamp was alien soil and nowhere in its precincts could Joe Breedlove find a man upon whom he might count.

Thinking of this, he shot a more interested glance at the gambler and for a brief moment he experienced hope. The gambler shifted slightly in his chair, meeting his glance and holding it a length of time. Comprehension passed between them. And yet even as hope flamed, it was pinched out; the gambler, in seeming idleness, passed a chip between his fingers, broke it squarely in twain and let the pieces fall. In a room crowded with lusting men, the gambler had delivered his message of futility. Dropping his head he remained a still, self-absorbed figure while a rising tide of passion swirled about him.

"Good man even so," Joe grimly told himself. "Like to know more of him."

And then the giant Flash had sprawled into the room and was standing passively waiting by the doors. The man known as Willy stiffened away from the bar, expectant. Black Clee's voice cut through the crowd. "Well, Mister Wise Gent, are you able to walk or do you want to be carried out to the horse?"

Joe saw a lane opening for him, the great Flash and the staring Willy waiting for him at the end of it. He turned to face the stove a moment, warming his hands; then in slow motion he swung about to face them all and walked to the door, the fine face thoughtfully set and the faint crust of silver shining around his temples. There was all about him a hush, and the stiff figures of the Lingard clan, hating him and watching for a break or flaw in his courage. Passing by, he met their faces, one by one; at the door he tarried to meet the crashing farewell of Black Clee.

"So-long, mister. You'll find the skids to hell greased by them that's gone before!"

But Joe shook his head. "For a man that's playin' with his own marked deck, your style is terrible. You press too hard. Always leave a sucker with a dollar and a smile."

Willy went through the doors and he followed, feeling the vast bulk of Flash tramping behind. Horses stood drearily in the rain and Willy's gun was against him. "Up in the saddle." A loop fell over his shoulders and clung loosely, nothing more than a warning and a guide; three abreast they turned eastward toward the street end.

"Down to my last white chip," Joe told himself. "The next run of cards had better be good. Yet I'm blamed if I can get it into my noggin that this is a plain cold-blooded Mexican execution. It don't seem real." Yet it seemed real enough in another moment. They were still in the street with window lights winking at them and calling them out of the dark. Willy rode close to the left with his gun muzzle resting forward on one thigh, hand holding the rope. Flash drew in slightly and fell a pace behind, upon which every fiber in Joe's body turned to metal. The man was already taking his butcher's station; already rehearsing the brutal business, with no little qualms to make him use the decency of the shadows to cloak his intent.

"You got a mile to go," muttered Joe.

"Why not ride up here and be sociable?"

Flash never spoke back. Willy muttered something in a queer voice and Joe swung that way to find the youth's face quite pallid in the gleam of out-thrown light. Willy's wide eyes were on Joe in fascinated horror and his teeth clicked audibly. "We ain't goin' to go no mile, by God!" he groaned. "We'll get it over with afore that or I'll duck and run!"

"Don't tell me you ain't used to this business," said Joe. "Black Clee is givin' you the post of honor."

"I'll do my part," said Willy with a faint doggedness, "but I ain't goin' to wait no mile. I ain't afraid — I'm plumb cold."

Joe's long suspended judgment woke and stabbed through this particular problem. The kid was sick at his stomach, terrified at a cold killing. Another three hundred yards and he'd be a bundle of nerves. Joe calculated coolly. Talk to the kid and keep him off a wire edge, make him forget his gun, then kick free and plunge over both horses, drawing Willy to the ground. Flash might get in a shot, which was a chance to take, but once he and the kid were wrestling against the earth the dumb-witted giant would be forced to dismount and grope. Time enough — maybe. The necessary breaks of luck had

277

to be with him; so thinking, he flexed his arm muscles against the binding loop and spoke casually.

"Well, life sort of keeps doublin' back on itself. Now I remember when I was about your age, in Abilene. There was a man named Hoggett — "

They cut past the last light of the town, burning beyond the last house. Wind whipped more strongly against them and runnels of water streamed down Joe's cheeks. Flash seemed to have disappeared and Joe only saw him by turning in the saddle and placing him against the town's glow. The movement put pressure on the rope and Willy's querulous, jumpy protest skittered into the storm. "Don't do that no more! Hold still or I'll — "

Joe became a taut, rigid figure; the chill of his bones dissolved before a sudden flash of fighter's hope. Looking back to discover the giant he had also seen a trio of horsemen cut around from the deep obscurity of the town and run over the background of lights into still other obscurity. His straining ears seemed to catch minute reverberations round about, faint runners of sound. He broke the spell with an effort at easy talk. "Why, if Black Clee's such a hound for trouble, should he take the time to tool me clean out in the prairie? A man's just as dead in Cowcamp as a mile beyond."

The slosh of riders was distinct to him and he thought it must surely warn the other two. Willy's answer came quickly as if he wanted to talk down the grisly fear inside him. "He don't want no killin' pinned on him. What happens out yonder in the sage brush ain't goin' to be traced back. See what I — "

The giant Flash bawled an indistinguishable word. Willy broke off his answer and yelled. Riders smashed in as Joe sagged Indian fashion below the rim of his saddle; and horses grunted with sudden impact. Indigo's half-wild summons rose above storm and turmoil. "Joe — hey, Joe!" A gun roared in Joe's ear and his horse stumbled down, leaving him at the bottom of the melee. He called up and recoiled from swirling hoofs. More voices and sharp profanity and the rip of metal against leather. It as all black confusion revolving around him for a short and dangerous space of time, but it swiftly split into twin whirlpools that drew away. Another shot raced along the wings of the wind and a mighty echo belched after it. Indigo was afoot, boots sloshing toward Joe.

"Joe — damn your soul — !"

"Here I am and don't damn a soul already

sold to Nick. How did you know — ”

“We was all stationed at the street and then we saw you bein’ herded out of the saloon. Not hurt any?”

“Nothing but my pride. You ain’t explained how you got to Cowcamp so blamed quick.”

“I wrung the necks offen them Lingards back at the house till one of ’em squawked that Black Clee’d taken most of his gang and come to town. I guessed if you’d been caught by some stray scout you’d be took right to Cowcamp. So I come.”

“And lost no time,” added Joe, rising from the earth. “I was beginnin’ to figure I’d have to write a will.” It was a good thing, he reflected, that Indigo couldn’t see the expression on his face. He struck the little partner’s chest and muttered, “You sure are a queer son-of-a-gun. Always wrong except at the right moment.”

“Well, you can leave the inquest till later. All the Marshalls are here. Now what? Them buzzards in town musta heard these two shots.”

“Might consider it was me bein’ drilled a little prematurely,” grunted Joe. “We’ll bank on that — ”

A voice came up. “That big man’s stone dead. Hit the ground like a ton o’ bricks. Flash Lingard, ain’t it? Well, there’s an end of a man that had two Marshalls to his credit. By God, I'd burn in brimstone eternally for the privilege o' killin' him a second time."

Joe heard Broderick Marshall's slightly burred speech. "Boys — boys, don't spread out so much. Where's those two fellows?"

"Say, I've got this other Lingard and he wants to tear the hide offen me!"

"Belt him on the nut and take his gun," snapped Indigo. "Got no time to herd anybody around now. Say the word, Joe."

"Where's an extra horse?" called Joe. "We'll lose no more time."

"Here — say, I can see some of 'em comin' out of the saloon!"

Joe fumbled for reins and stirrup, swung up and spoke coolly. "All here? Indigo, take about four of the boys and stick right up at the end of the street. I'm goin' down the back alley with the rest and bust into the saloon from behind. When they come out the front let 'em have it. Might send one man around to the rear of the stable. Let's go. Nothin' complicated about this. Stick to the shadows and sling it into 'em. Come on — "

He spurred off, swinging a little wide of the street's beckoning mouth. He heard the Marshalls pounding behind and the welcome squeal of leather. Men were in Cowcamp's street and fiddling with the racked ponies, but they seemed to be taking their own good time and without suspicion. Full on, Joe hit the back lots, checked in a trifle, and pounded past the shadowed hips of the row of tenements. A burst of firing rose over the roofs, announcing Indigo's premature enthusiasm. Joe swore and tore into the tricky area, heedless of whatever debris might lay there to unhorse him. Somebody, trying to cut out of the single column and come abreast, smashed into trouble and went cursing from the saddle.

They were at the saloon's rear. A door stood open, a yellow rectangle of light cutting the black wall. Somebody catapulted out of it, caught himself with a half scream of discovery and clawed for his gun. There was a double blast and the man sagged down, body half inside and half outside the place. Joe sprang from his horse, elbowing ahead of the eager Marshalls. A dozen voices cried out and the pressure of their haste threw Joe full into the room. The stink of kerosene swirled along it, coming from lamps abruptly shattered; in the semidarkness Joe's sweeping glance saw only a few men — one poised at the front door and trying desperately to crowd through, some behind the bar, and the gambler still sitting at his table. Joe shouted a warning.

"Watch that bar! Never mind the man at the table — let him alone." And then the room was a-roar with the detonating blasts of gun play, and sprays of glass from the great plate-mirror behind the bar went jangling to the floor, the poor light sparkling on it fitfully. Joe flung himself at the mahogany barrier, crying at the gambler, "Get down on the floor and stay there!" Powder belched in his face as he cut around the bar and found three men crouched there, beaten down by the Marshalls' flinging bullets. A cry of surrender came to him; Marshalls swarmed over the barrier and dropped atop those cowering Lingards and then a yell of heady triumph came from one of them.

"We can lick these bastards!"

"One man stick here," said Joe, wheeling for the door. "Come on!"

The firing in the street increased in fury. The saloon's swinging panels rocked with the impact of lead, causing Joe to throw up his arm in warning. "Half of you cut around the back alley and come into the street from the west end. Rest stay with me. Put out all the lights except behind the bar. Break down the windows."

"How about the second floor of this joint?"

"Try it, but be careful." Joe swung a chair

through a window, splintering glass and sash in one great blow. Nobody stood on the street in front of him and so, with a summons to the rest of the Marshalls, he jumped through and flattened himself against the wall. Lingards were racing over the street to the stable, deserting any attack they might have debated on the saloon. Black Clee's strangled challenge sounded farther to the east, in Indigo's direction, and then was cut off by an irregular roar of freshly roused guns. Slugs began to beat the wall beside him, and his eyes caught the purplish jetting of a muzzle flame directly opposite. He fired, sidled away, and fired again. A Marshall coming out of the window pitched forward with a suppressed groan. "I took one in the laig, by God! Watch out!"

Joe stood still, orienting the main point of attack. The Lingards were scattered all over the town, burrowing into this building and that one. But the bulk of them seemed to have taken to the stable; and there was another small sputter of resistance over by the restaurant. Indigo had advanced down the street and was trying to smother that; and from the opposite end Joe saw the Marshall flanking party come along hurriedly. Gun shots began to play around from the second story of the saloon, directly overhead.

Broderick Marshall ran ahead of the party from the west, and sang out drunkenly, "Where they at — where the yella dogs gone?"

"We've got to throw a ring around that stable," said one. "You take your boys back of it and watch the rear doors. We'll peck away from the front."

Broderick Marshall wheeled obediently and hurried off. A glow of light began shimmering out of the stable opening and before Joe had time to do more than discover it, a tremendous core of fire flashed inside and began to roar.

"On fire!"

"Come on back here!" yelled Joe and reached to get the gun of the Marshall at his feet. The Lingards in the stable came stumbling out in a compact body, crossing directly for their horses tethered in front of the saloon, each man tragically outlined by the sweep of flames at his back. "Good God," muttered Joe and stepped around to command a better vista. He opened up rapidly and saw a renegade buckle up and go sprawling. Indigo's party was racing in at full speed and Broderick Marshall had turned to close the other jaw of the vise. Up on the roof of the saloon porch the Marshall marksmen were pouring a steady stream of lead into the desperate Lingard foray; and for one swirling, terrific minute the beat and roar of the guns overwhelmed every other sound of the night. Horses broke clear of the rack. The Lingards, reaching that rack, formed a mad mass of animals and men. A rider, gone berserk, flung himself out of the confusion and spurred directly down on Indigo's party; Joe saw the man career out of his saddle. The horse smashed swiftly on.

Joe's shrewd reason told him then the Lingard rule was ended. These men had run their race; their pride of clan was destroyed. Nothing but demoralization reigned among the melee of curvetting, half-mad horses and cursing, half-mad men. Indigo's party was up; Broderick Marshall's party was up. The jaws of the vise had closed and in the guttering light from the stable the Lingards were fatally exposed. Some of them had their horses under control but dared not mount and become fair targets. Others crouched and tried to fire over saddle rims. Men were down, men were creeping in broken fashion out of the bloody area. Joe called commandingly to them. "Pitch up, Lingards! Pitch up and quit!"

"Let 'em die!" roared Broderick Marshall. "That's what they'd do to us!"

"Stop that! Pitch up and quit, Lingards!

No more slaughter."

"A fair chance?" one of the Lingards yelled back.

"You'll take your chances," was Joe's grim reply. "But we ain't Indian-hearted. Pitch up before we blast you off the street."

The firing had died; a pair of arms showed above a pony's back. Both parties stood rigid, waiting sullenly for a break. Joe's soft drawl smoothed down the suspense. "No use in cold killin'. Stiffen out your elbows — every last one of you. This fight's over. Marshall, I want no Mexican executions, you hear that? You've paid off the bill. Put up those arms — walk out from the horses." As he spoke he saw the Lingards complying one by one with the order. Indigo's high-pitched voice broke in. "I'll pull them stingers, Joe. Step this way one by one, you buzzards."

Joe walked over to get a better view of them. The roar of the stable blaze reached a crackling tempo and great gusts of flame poured out of the openings; as they watched, a section of roof sagged and then a licking banner of red sheared the sky. The rain began to steam and sputter and the heat grew uncomfortable in the street. Joe had to raise his words to a higher pitch. "Get these horses out of the way! Where's Black Clee?"

Nobody answered him. A woman ran from a building beyond the stable and a roll of bedding fell out of the saloon's highest window. Joe saw a man race from the restaurant across the street to the general store. On impulse he galloped away from the crowd and closed in. By the fast strengthening fire light he saw the sign on the store front: *Clee Lingard, Merchandise.* And as he threw himself into the place he drew his gun.

There was a man tearing out a till behind the counter, back turned: a man cursing at every rise and fall of his breath; a man raging greedily at the money he pawed out of the receptacle. He seemed deaf and blind to all else and not until he stuffed his pockets full did he turn to discover Joe standing there. There was a shine of sweat on Black Clee's cheekbones and a ragged smear of blood on one wrist. He pulled himself back, lips spreading clear of great white teeth; all the deadly temper of the man flared up to his jet eyes and flashed against Joe.

"My town — burnin' to the ground!" he cried. "Damn your soul, hell ain't hot enough for you! My town — you understand that?"

"What about your men lyin' dead on the street — what about the Marshalls gone and the widows made? What about that, Lingard?"

"What do I care about men?" shouted the renegade. "I make 'em and I break 'em and there's always more to get. But I'll kill you for burnin' my town! I had ought to have done it long ago in the river shanty! I'm bringin' down the black curse on your head — "

"Either quit or draw," droned Joe and waited a long, long time. The snarl of the spreading fire was filling his ears and the flicker of it made leaping patterns through the store. Black Clee's chest trembled and the eyes of the man seemed to grow large with strain. He moved, wrenched away; his arm fell and rose. Almost critically Joe watched the fellow's muscles playing. The lamp on the counter jumped violently to an explosion and Indigo came racing out of the street to cry, "What's goin' on here?" Joe's spare figure was immobile in the center of the room. Powder smoke curled faintly from the muzzle of a loose gun, and Black Clee's bulk lay curved over the counter, dark face congested with stopped blood.

"A sure-thing artist," muttered Joe, "but poor at gamblin'. He never knew how to play in a pinch. Always leave a sucker with a smile, Indigo, or the sucker may return someday to squawk. Let's get out of here."

"This joint ain't goin' to be nothin' but

ashes in an hour from now," opined Indigo. "What next?"

The Marshalls had driven the Lingard captives into the saloon and lighted some of the smashed lamps. Broderick Marshall stood at the bar, absorbed in unpleasant thoughts. He roused himself at Joe's entry, to share his troubles. "I ain't prepared to hold all these men. What am I goin' to do?"

But Joe's attention was diverted to a table in the center of the room. The gambler sat in a chair by it, head and shoulders fallen forward and white fingers lying nerveless before him. Joe walked over, seeing a pocket pistol lying flat against the green surface. A pack of cards had been sorted and the jack of spades lay face up with a single white chip on it. The man was dead by his own act. Joe turned grimly away.

"A better man than any Lingard in town. He had a conscience — and it killed him."

Broderick Marshall was speaking fretfully. "I ain't a judge and jury and I ain't goin' to establish no prison. Where's Black Clee?"

"Dead," said Joe briefly. "You've busted the back of his family, or I'm no prophet."

"We ain't goin' to get nowhere tryin' to take 'em to jail," pursued Broderick Marshall.

"They'd be out in thirty days and there's our trip for nothin'. Any of you heavy-handed thieves and cutthroats pinin' for more trouble?"

"This joint's burnin' up," broke in a Lingard. "You goin' to stand by and let us lose all our belongings?"

"I'm askin' if any of you want to carry on this crap?" insisted Broderick Marshall. But there was no answer. The old man thought a while longer. "Then I'll say this: from now on there's a deadline at the base of the ridge. Any Lingard caught over it will die. Lonesome Valley is Marshall country. Stay out of it. You — and you — and you," pointing to five of the older Lingards, "are out of it. Fog out of this country as quick as the Lord will let you. Stay, and we'll come and hunt you down. My advice to the rest of you is to walk mighty humble. Marshalls' turn to have the upper hand a while. You have done us plenty of grief, but we don't go in for promiscuous robbery and bushwhackin'. I'm takin' all your horses back with me tonight. I'm takin' provisions from the store. Any objections?"

"Who pays for that?" queried a Lingard.

"When Black Clee renders a bill," was the old man's grim reply, "we'll honor it. Not before. Boys — go down to the store and collect all you can carry in the saddle."

Joe walked out to the street, with Indigo behind. The little partner pointed to some horses herded up at the west end. "Our brutes are yonder. I saw 'em."

"Let's get out of this before that roof falls on top of us," said Joe. "Sort of hate to see fire lick up a town. Lot of sweat and hopes went into those buildings."

Indigo snorted derisively. "You got a great call to get soft-hearted, considerin' all that's happened."

"Any Marshalls killed?" asked Joe anxiously.

"I dunno," grunted Indigo. "Couple took lead in 'em. That's about all I know — "

Joe stopped in his tracks. A rider rounded into the street, shrouded in a black slicker, and rode toward them. A supple body swayed with the horse and a white face looked at them.

"Ma'am," said Joe, "what you doin' here?"

The woman with the copper-colored hair checked in and looked down, grave eyes absorbing Joe, seeming to inspect every feature of the man. She bent from the saddle and touched his shoulder. "I had to come," said she slowly, each word falling deliberately. "You're not hurt?"

"Like the wanderin' Jew, I'll go on forever," muttered Joe. He had taken off his hat and the rain streamed down the lean face. "This night sees the end of your troubles. You will never be bothered by Clee Lingard again."

"I knew my troubles were ended," said she slowly, "when you came into our house. My friend, have you always been sad?"

"I do not believe in a man pitying himself," mumbled Joe.

"Put on your hat. You'll catch cold. You're coming back to our place to sleep tonight, aren't you?"

He looked past her to the fitful sky. "Day ain't so far off. The Marshalls will have some accountin' to make and maybe some grievin' to do. No, my partner and me had better take the trail home."

He saw disappointment cross her fine, clear face. "But you will come back sometime?"

He looked directly at her, body stiffening. "I'll be back."

"You will find me waiting to see you," she said quietly. For a little while longer these two grave, straight people stood face to face. The pressure of her hand increased on his shoulder and then was withdrawn. She lifted the reins and the pony turned; in a few moments she was lost from their sight in the blackness of the rain-swept night.

Joe thoughtfully swung up on his pony, turned to Indigo and said, "Let's hit the trail for home."

Ernest Haycox during his lifetime was considered the dean among authors of Western fiction. When the Western Writers of America was first organized in 1953, what became the Golden Spur Award for outstanding achievement in writing Western fiction was first going to be called the "Erny" in homage to Haycox. He was born in Portland, Oregon and, while still an undergraduate at the University of Oregon in Eugene, sold his first short story to the OVERLAND MONTHLY. His name soon became established in all the leading pulp magazines of the day, including Street and Smith's WESTERN STORY MAGAZINE and Doubleday's WEST MAGAZINE. His first novel, FREE GRASS, was published in book form in 1929. In 1931 he broke into the pages of COLLIER'S and from that time on was regularly featured in this magazine, either with a short story or a serial that was later published as a novel. In the 1940s his serials began appearing in THE SATURDAY EVENING POST and it was there that modern classics such as BUGLES IN THE AFTERNOON (1944) and CANYON PASSAGE (1945) were first published. Both of these novels were also made into major motion pictures although, perhaps, the film most loved and remembered is STAGECOACH (United Artists, 1939) directed by John Ford and starring John Wayne, based on Haycox's short story "Stage to Lordsburg." No history of the Western story in the 20th Century would be possible without reference to Haycox's fiction and his tremendous influence on other writers of stature, such as Peter Dawson, Norman A. Fox, Wayne D. Overholser, and Luke Short, among many. During his last years, before his premature death from abdominal carcinoma, he set himself the task of writing historical fiction which he felt would provide a fitting legacy and the consummation of his life's work. He almost always has an involving story to tell and one in which there is something not so readily definable that raises it above its time, an image possibly, a turn of phrase, or even a sensation, the smell of dust after rain or the solitude of an Arizona night. Haycox was an author whose Western fiction has made an abiding contribution to world literature.